# *Revenge*

## *A Novel*

### *by*
### *Veronica West*

PublishAmerica

Baltimore

First printing

ISBN: 1-4137-3367-0
PUBLISHED BY PUBLISHAMERICA, LLLP
www.publishamerica.com
Baltimore

Printed in the United States of America

*In loving memory of my mother,*
*Elvia Keulen.*

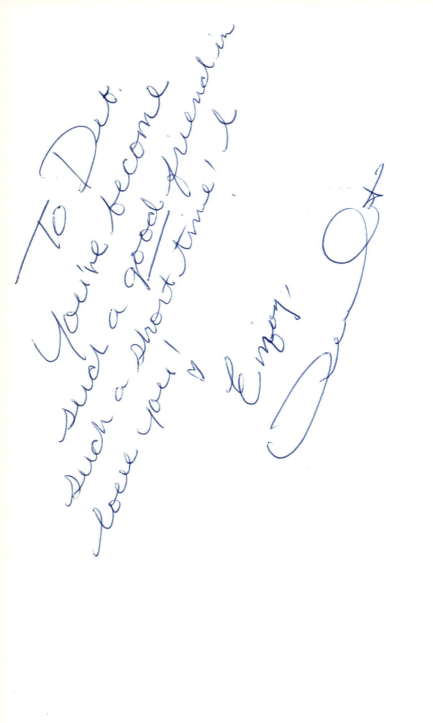

To Dee.
You've become
such a good friend in
such a short time! I
love you!

Enjoy!

# *Acknowledgements:*

There are so many things I want to say and people to mention and thank. I feel so blessed that I have a circle of family and friends who truly love me. You all know who you are and know that *I love you* as well.

I would first like to thank Publish America from the very bottom of my heart for their faith in me, and for making my dream become a reality. Thank you so much.

For my loving husband, Scott, my life partner, lover, and friend...whose faith I can always count on. I love you.

For my three beautiful children; Hayden, Austin and Taylor, you are the brightest lights in my life and the one perfect thing I have and will have *ever* done...I love you as high as the sky and as deep as the sea.

For my family; my wonderful father, Fred; sisters, Johanna and Sandy; and my brother, Patrick. You are my blood. The finest people I will ever know. Your love, faith, and support for me, and *of* me, are unwavering and final. As is mine. Enough said....

My sister-in-law, Lorin, so close to my heart. We will always have Palm Springs, girl!

My brother-in-laws, John, Vern and David, you guys are the greatest.

My dear nephews and nieces, I love you all so *very* much.

Jackie and Cliff you both mean the *world* to me.

Terry and Sally I treasure the *special* times we share.

I love you all....

Mother...I know you are in heaven doing God's work. I feel you every day, and I will *miss* you until the day I die. Please continue to look after and protect your children and their spouses, your grandchildren and Daddy.

Te amo, Mommy....

Peace and Love...
*Veronica*

# Chapter One

## New York City

Eric Robinson was running for his life. His breath was whistling past his lips and the pain in his side felt like someone held a hot poker to it.

He heard hard, fast footsteps behind him, and thought, *SHIT...he's running like a madman.*

He quickly glanced back and lost his balance. He turned his ankle over painfully and landed flat on his back. He managed to stagger to his feet. Breathing heavily, he winced and hunched over, hanging his head between his knees.

"It's all over Eric."

The sound of the deep, gravely voice caused Eric's knees to buckle. He had to fight to keep from vomiting.

"Get the fuck away from me!" he shrieked.

Dominic Lockwood stared down at him. "Did you really think you'd get away with it?"

The man smiled a wide toothy grin that was so frightening that Eric shuddered violently.

"You *owe* me, Robinson. More than you know. You're gonna *wish* you were dead."

Eric dropped to his knees and threw up.

"And I intend to collect," said Dominic, completely ignoring the disgusting, retching sounds.

Everything was falling in to place, just as he had planned. He had counted on Robinson's greed to help him seek the revenge that he had thirsted for years to get.

He lived and breathed it.

And now that the wheels were in motion, there was no stopping them.

"Whaddaya want from me, you son of a bitch? There's nothing I have now that you could possibly want."

Dominic laughed low-down and dark. It was truly an evil sound. "Really? Well, *I* can think of something."

"What?" Eric's voice trembled despite his efforts to keep it steady. Hatred, deep-seated and terrifying, seemed to permeate around him like a dark poisonous cloud.

Dominic's eyes bored into Eric's unflinchingly, all traces of laughter obliterated. "It's *whom*...I want Anna."

Eric narrowed his eyes, "Anna? How do you know about *her*...?

He laughed incredulously. "You think I'm just gonna hand my wife over to you?"

"Yes. That's *exactly* what you're going to do."

"What do you want *her* for anyway? She's nothin' but a user man, she'll screw you over in a New York minute."

The brilliant high beams of a black SUV interrupted Eric as it roared up alongside Dominic.

Eric's gut clenched in fear. His eyes cut back and forth from Lockwood to the three-hundred-pound monster lumbering out of the car.

The dude was a huge, mean-looking Italian with beady black eyes and a sneer.

Lockwood had Eric's balls nailed to the floor, and he knew it. He put a shaking hand to his head. *Jesus Christ, Anna's gonna freak when she finds out.*

Eric couldn't remember the last time that he told his wife that he loved her. He certainly wouldn't be winning any husband of the year awards, that was for sure.

He screwed anything in a skirt and hit her when he drank. He forgot birthdays, anniversaries, and gambled on a regular basis.

He also had a nice little coke habit that had him in debt to Johnny "The Rat" Falcone, a loan shark with a real mean streak.

The thud of a zippered bag landing on the car's sleek black hood snapped Eric out of his unhappy reverie.

"What's in the bag?" he asked nervously. His pulse was visibly pounding in his throat.

"That depends on you."

Dominic reached down, yanked Eric upright and pulled his face to within inches of his own. "There's the quarter of a million dollars that you stole, along with a loaded Beretta."

He paused to observe the fear and avarice in the other man's eyes. "You have two choices and somehow I think you'll like my second choice a whole lot better. Your first choice is that I pull the piece out and blow your fuckin' brains all over the pavement. After all, there's no Judge or jury in this country who'd convict me for exterminating a shitty little cockroach like you."

"Listen," Eric interrupted desperately. "Ya gotta believe me, it was all Anna's idea, she was the brains behind everything, I swear it! She's a cold, calculating bitch. She…"

"Or," Dominic went on ignoring Eric. "You can skip town with the money and save your cowardly ass."

Dominic's eyes were locked on Eric's, daring him to speak.

It didn't even take him a heartbeat to answer.

"I'll take the money," he whispered greedily, not caring that he basically bartered his wife to another man.

"That's a real good choice Robinson. You're not so stupid after all." He leaned over Eric and whispered slyly. "You know, I gotta tell ya…I can't wait to get Anna in to my bed."

"You lousy son of a bitch," Eric growled. He closed his eyes and wished he never uttered the words because, in a flash, Dominic unzipped the bag and pulled the gun out.

"What an ungrateful asshole you are," he replied with a slight smile on his face.

He casually took aim, pulled the trigger twice, and grazed both of Eric's legs.

Eric screamed in agony, clutching his legs close to his chest.

"Don't be such a pussy. They're only flesh wounds. You'll be walking in a coupla days," said Dominic unsympathetically.

"You're fuckin' crazy man! I won't cause any trouble…I'll disappear, I promise, just please put the gun away."

"I'd like to trust you, but how do I know you won't try and crawl back into town like the scum you are?" Dominic asked with the innocence of a cobra, all the while pointing the weapon at his enemy's shriveled balls.

"Jesus Christ!" screeched Eric. "I swear to you, you'll never hear from me again. Please…I'm beggin', man!" He started to cry in earnest while clutching his injured legs closely to his chest.

Dominic threw the open bag down at Eric's feet, and then spoke for the first time to the silent man standing next to him. "Take this piece of shit over to Johansen. Tell him to fix him up. Then accompany our fucked-up friend on his plane ride. I'm sure you'll explain the consequences, if he decides to show his face."

The man grinned and nodded. He specialized in consequences.

Dominic took one last look at Robinson scooping up the fallen money all around him. Sweat ran down his pasty face in rivulets as he frantically shoved the money back into the bag. He looked at him with contempt.

"Oh, and Paulie," he called to the burly bodyguard. "Make sure Johansen doesn't give him anything to kill the pain."

That being said, Dominic turned around, and strolled out of the garage into the fresh night air.

He was in complete and total control.

The game was just beginning. He would make Eric Robinson pay a thousand times over for Jenny's death. Of that there was no doubt.

# Chapter Two

Anna Robinson was a beautiful woman. Petite and slender; she had jet-black hair falling in shiny ripples down her back, ending just above her tailbone.

All that silky hair was the perfect frame for the thickly lashed, ice-blue eyes that dominated her perfect oval face. Her mother called them cat's eyes. At the moment, the last thing on her mind was her looks.

She was emotionally and physically drained. The last few months had been like a nightmare she couldn't wake up from. Her husband had left her, and he didn't even have the decency to tell her to her face.

Instead, Eric left her a lame note filled with stupid platitudes. Such as, *"I'm doing you a favor by leaving you," "you deserve better than me,"* or worse yet. *"The men are gonna line up just to get a crack at you."*

*Yeah, right.* Anna thought sourly.

The only men who were going to walk into her life were the bill collectors and the loan sharks demanding their money. He had left her with a mountain of bills and no possible way to pay them back.

She shuddered to think of the impending visit from Eric's so-called "gambling buddies," who in reality were vicious loan sharks who made it crystal clear that she could work her debt off, if she so desired.

Since prostitution wasn't her idea of a career choice. It was time to start liquidating and quickly. She wearily ran her slender fingers

11

through her hair when the shrill ring of the telephone nearly caused her to jump out of her skin.

"Hello?"

"Pay up, bitch."

There was a sharp click, then a dial tone. Anna stared down at the phone in shock, paralyzed with fear. She gently put the phone on its nest without really knowing it, and turned and walked toward the bedroom like a zombie.

She crossed the room and went directly to her jewelry box. With trembling fingers, she pulled out three velvet boxes. The first box contained a heart-shaped diamond necklace that Eric had given her shortly after they were married.

She supposed she was lucky that he didn't pawn them, which was exactly what she would have to do. Inside the second box were the small diamond earrings that her mother bought her when she graduated high school.

She gazed at the final items, her engagement ring and wedding band. Her eyes slowly filled with tears, she thought when she took her vows, it would be forever.

What a fool she was.

She snapped the box shut, picked up the other two and headed out the front door. Outside, she took a few gulps of air to brace herself, then climbed inside her old VW and chugged off down the quiet street. Anna wasn't even aware that Dominic Lockwood was following her.

## Chapter Three

Dominic settled himself comfortably against the plush leather seat of his black Jaguar. He was parked across the street from a gaudy red, green and white building appropriately called Chewy's Pawn Shop.

She'd been in there for a few moments, he mused, chewing on his inner lip. He was going to make his move tonight. He knew that she was getting desperate. The paltry trinkets she was pawning right at this moment wouldn't add up to a fraction of what she needed.

He smiled to himself when he recalled his visit with Johnny the Rat. He strode into the cockroach-infested hovel that passed for the loan shark's office, and saw the man himself seated behind a battered desk, with a fat Cuban cigar poking obscenely between his thick lips.

"Who the fuck are ya, and whaddaya want?"

Johnny the Rat was not a warm and fuzzy person.

"Call your dogs off of Anna Robinson."

"Drop dead, ya piece a shit or I'll have your ass for breakfast, who the fuck d'ya think…" Johnny's tirade stopped midstream when Dominic pulled out an envelope from the breast pocket of his immaculate Armani suit. It landed with a loud thud on the filthy, grime-encrusted desk.

Johnny opened the envelope and let out a gleeful whoop, "There must be…"

"There's fifty thousand dollars," interrupted Dominic harshly, hating the disgusting little rodent more as the seconds ticked by. "Anna Robinson is no longer in debt to you," he said tightly, staring him down through steely gray slits.

13

"What? Are ya bangin' her?" he asked with a nasty smirk on his face. "I don't blame you, my friend. I hear she's one tight little piece of…"

Johnny was taken completely by surprise when Dominic Lockwood's fist connected with a vengeance on the fleshy blob that once was his nose.

"Let's get one thing straight," snarled Lockwood, his face hovering centimeters above the bloody face of Johnny Falcone. "I'm *not* your friend and Mrs. Robinson is no longer your problem, so if I catch you or your dogs anywhere *near* her, I'll peel your skin off in strips and shove 'em up your ass. Now…do we understand each other?"

"All right, all *right* already, I got my money. Just get the *hell* outta here!" Frankly, Johnny had enough of this disrespectful shit. The dude had on fancy clothes but didn't disguise the fact that he was dangerous, and Johnny had enough bullshit going on in his life. He just wanted this asshole out of his office.

"Gladly," Dominic muttered. "The stink in here makes my stomach turn. Why don't you invest a coupla bucks and get yourself some mouthwash. Your breath smells like a septic tank."

He almost laughed outright when the image of the lambasted loan shark's face loomed before him. Abruptly dismissing Johnny from his world, he turned his attention back to Anna Robinson.

Unbeknownst to her, he just this morning paid each and every one of the creditors that the Robinsons had owed. Amazing how cold, hard cash influenced all people, Dominic thought cynically.

Once they knew they were getting paid, they conveniently asked zero questions. Assuring him no further contact with Mrs. Robinson would be necessary.

Dominic walked out owning Anna, and he relished seeing her in person tonight. He was holding all the cards and would let no one forget it.

sat opposite him on the sofa. The seconds ticked by with complete silence between them.

His face was half-covered in shadow, but his eyes tracked her every move, and if that wasn't unnerving enough, he was as still as a statue. She sensed his relaxed demeanor was deliberate, because his eyes were as sharp as stilettos and fixated on her.

She was sure if she made a sudden dash for the front door, he would have sprung up like a panther and stopped her dead in her tracks. The unnatural silence stretched on as she took in his face.

His hair was long, straight, and as black as coal. It ended just below his shoulders. It wasn't a look many men could carry off, but it suited him perfectly. It was thick, healthy, and superbly cut.

Glossy eyebrows rested regally above his metallic gray eyes. A ring of black rimed the light irises, giving them the hard look of a wolf.

He had a strong face with a square jaw, and a sensual mouth. A perfectly manicured mustache and goatee gave him a dark, exotic look. His nose had been broken, leaving a slight bump across the bridge. His face was too hard for anyone to call him a pretty boy, but it had immense character. He was incredibly handsome.

Dangerously so.

The black cashmere topcoat that he wore was of the finest money could buy, and from what she could see of his suit, it too must have cost a fortune.

Anna suddenly realized how intently she was staring. It also occurred to her that he was staring just as intently at her. His eyes were watchful...predatory.

"Had a good look?"

"Why are you here?" she asked abruptly, her cheeks rosy with embarrassment.

He lifted an imperious brow. "You and your husband screwed me out of two-hundred and fifty-thousand dollars, and I want compensation," he answered coolly, his gray eyes glinting with feral lights.

To say that she was stunned was putting it mildly. Her stomach dropped to her feet and it was all she could do to keep herself from throwing up on his handmade Italian shoes.

"I beg your pardon…?" she asked faintly.

"I don't think there's anything wrong with your hearing, Anna," he chided.

"Do you have my money?" he asked pleasantly, knowing full well that she didn't.

"I…I'm sorry Mr. Lockwood, but up until ten minutes ago, I never even knew that you existed!"

"Bullshit," he rapped out. "You still haven't answered my question. Can you make good on the debt?"

Nothing in his face was sympathetic to her plight.

"No, of course not! I have *exactly* sixty-two hundred dollars to my name. Where on earth would I get that kind of money from?" She was panicking and her heart was thrumming so loud she was sure he could hear it.

He shrugged his shoulders. "Beats me, your type *always* seems to land on their feet. You've got big problems though. Johnny Falcone is a nasty little worm that wouldn't mind getting his hands on your money," he snickered unpleasantly. "And on other things as well."

"How do you know my personal affairs? What are you, some kind of lunatic going around spying on total strangers? You had better leave *now,* Mr. Lockwood, before my husband comes home!"

"Now *you're* the one who's sounding like the lunatic, Anna. Your *ex*-husband," he stressed. "Isn't coming home tonight or any other night and you know it. So you can drop the innocent babe in the woods act, because I can see right through it. You're nothing but a liar and *just* as much of a user as Eric is."

Anna suddenly grew very still and stared at him through frightened blue eyes. He *was* dangerous and sinister.

"I have *no* idea what you're talking about. I don't *know* you; I don't *want* to know you. You're insane. You didn't come here to talk to me at all. You came here for a reason, and not just for money that my *husband,*" she now stressed the word, "supposedly owes you. So just tell me what it is you came here for."

Dominic stared at her; a faint smile was on his lips. "You. You're what I came here for," he replied chillingly.

"You see, I *own* you, Anna. Just ask Johnny and all those bloodthirsty bill collectors I paid off. You're leaving here with me tonight."

Dominic leaned slightly forward to observe the shock, disbelief, and fear that raced across her face from the bombshell he just dropped. "Since you don't have my money, I'll just have to think of another way for you to repay me..." He paused to insolently peruse her breasts, "know what I mean?"

"You're crazy..." Anna whispered in a high, thin voice.

She abruptly jumped to her feet as the enormity of what he was saying hit home.

Turning, she started to streak towards the front door when he was upon her like a wild animal, grabbing her slender shoulders and pressing her up against the rough stucco wall of the sitting room.

Her breathing was harsh and rapid, and her heart was banging hard against her ribs. She felt light-headed and faint.

Dominic laced his fingers behind her neck and drew her so close that their lips almost touched.

"Listen to me carefully because I'm only going to say this *once*," he rasped softly.

"I paid a *lot* of money to some very unpleasant people, Anna. Johnny was looking forward to pimping you out to every freak with a little cash in his pocket. And that's after he had you for himself. The way *I* see it, I did you a favor. But I can also undo it in a heartbeat and throw you back to the wolves. You make the choice."

Anna stared wide-eyed at him. Terror and anger were warring for supremacy. "Why are you *doing* this to me? You don't even *know* me, and you sure as hell don't *own* me! I'm not something that can be bought or sold. I didn't ask you to pay my debts for me, so the way *I* see it, I don't owe you a *damn* thing, you son of a bitch! I'll get away from you the first chance I get!"

Dominic glared at her. "I knew you'd show your true self sooner or later. You have no *idea* of who I am or what I can do to you. I can make your life a living hell." Dominic tightened his hold on her neck. "And believe me, sweetheart, I've got the money and power to do it."

Anna choked back the tears that were threatening to burst through. "I won't let you *do this* to me, you bastard!" Her fists were banging against the rock-hard wall of his chest.

Dominic caught her wrists as easily as he would a child's. "Would you rather be in Johnny's debt? Because that can be arranged, trust me. Shall I call him up and make him your problem again?"

Dominic released her and walked to the little antique table, picking up the phone, pretending to call.

"Wait…" Anna whispered, tears damming over her beautiful eyes.

She put a shaking hand to her forehead. For the time being, this man had control over her life. She needed to think…to formulate some course of action to get her out of this horrible situation.

"That won't be necessary. I'll do as you ask," she said stiffly.

A cold smile spread across Dominic's face. "I'm *so* glad that you changed your mind," he said sarcastically. "Get your purse, and let's go."

# *Chapter Five*

## *The Past*

Dominic Joseph Lockwood was born in The Bronx Municipal Hospital thirty-four years ago. It should have been a joyous event, but the Lockwood house was not a happy one.

They were dirt poor and lived in a rough neighborhood. Dominic and his younger sister, Jenny, grew up both fearing and hating their abusive, alcoholic father, Joseph Lockwood.

Through their turbulent years growing up, the only love and affection the children ever received was from their frail mother, Abigail. At fourteen, Dominic was six feet tall and built like an eighteen-year-old. He was as tough as nails and cynical beyond his years. Living the way he did hardened him to such a degree that any trace of the carefree child he should have been was completely erased.

He lost track of the times that he'd gotten his ass kicked walking home from school by gang members and bullies. He learned at a young age to fight dirty and win.

At home it was a different story.

His father ruled the house with an iron fist. His children and wife, Abigail, were nothing to him but objects that he could abuse.

Abigail's spirit had long ago been crushed to nothing by the years of mental and physical torment he heaped upon her. Joseph took sadistic pleasure in humiliating his wife in any way he could.

He often would tell her how stupid and ugly she was, and what an uptight, frigid bitch she was in bed. On a lucky day that was all she had to endure. But throw a bottle of liquor into the mix and she became his personal punching bag.

Dominic loathed his father with a blinding passion. He and his sister fared no better than their mother did. Dominic took the beatings intended for Jenny countless times. He could not bear the thought of his gentle sister being harmed, so when he knew his father was going after her, he'd deliberately say or do something to divert his attention to himself.

He'd get in between his mother and Joseph, and he paid dearly for it. He fantasized daily about his father getting hit by a bus, or mugged by the hoods that roamed the rundown projects where they lived.

Anything to keep the rotten bastard away from his mother and Jenny. He didn't deserve a wife and kids. His dear old dad could never hold down a steady job for more than a month. If it wasn't for welfare, they would have lived on the street.

There was never any money for decent clothes, and they were lucky if there was food in the refrigerator by the end of the week. He wished he had the power to just run away, taking his beloved mother and sister with him. He'd give them the kind of life they deserved. But it was never going to happen.

**\*\*\*\*\*\*\*\*\*\***

When Dominic was seventeen, he came home from school to a silent home. That was strange, because his mother should have been there. He made his way through the cramped apartment with its cheap, mismatched furniture and yellow-stained walls.

The dismal sight never failed to burn in his stomach like acid. His mother tried so hard to keep the apartment neat as a pin and cheery, but the place was a dump, and there was nothing that could change that fact.

His heart started knocking against his ribs, and the hairs on his arms stood on end. Something was terribly wrong, he could feel it instinctively. The bathroom door at the end of the hall was almost closed.

Dominic pushed gently with his fingertips until it swung open. His breath left his body in one painful rush. He stood horrified trying to make sense of what he was seeing.

Dominic sank to his knees and stayed there transfixed with grief. A small choking sound escaped him.

His beautiful mother was floating in bloody water, one slashed wrist dangling over the rusty tub.

The years of desolation and abuse had finally been too much for Abigail. She was too weak in spirit to even live for her children, and tragically, she felt ending her life was the only way to escape Joseph's tyranny.

He rose to his feet unsteadily and stared down at her with tear-filled eyes.

"Mom," he whispered brokenly.

He picked her up out of the tub and gently laid her on her bed. He didn't want Jenny to see their mother the way he had. He dried her off and put on her one good dress. He smoothed her hair, placed her rosary in her hand, and knelt by her bed.

Then he wept until he had no tears left.

Something died forever inside Dominic that day. He and Jenny alone took care of the funeral arrangements. No one could locate Joseph to tell him of his wife's suicide. It was not unusual for him to go on week-long benders.

Dominic and his sister were the only mourners present when their mother was buried. His sister was all he had left now. He didn't think it could get any worse.

He was wrong.

**\*\*\*\*\*\*\*\*\*\***

His father showed no signs of grief whatsoever over the death of his wife. He still continued his drinking, screwing, and gambling as if nothing had happened. If Dominic had owned a gun, he would have blown his head off in a heartbeat. He dreamed of beating him slowly to death.

Jenny, his beautiful sister, was the image of Abigail. Her brown hair curled around her delicate, heart-shaped face the same way her mother's did. She had brown doe's eyes with long, thick lashes and a rosebud mouth.

At age sixteen, she was already blossoming in to a lovely young woman. The neighborhood boys knew better than to try a move on Jenny Lockwood. Dominic turned into a wild animal if one of them so much as tried to start a conversation with her.

Lockwood's tough reputation preceded him, and many punks had gone home black and blue over his sister.

There was no way that Jenny would wind up with any one of those losers, he thought fiercely. He would take them apart piece by piece if they even tried to get in her orbit.

His gentle, innocent sister deserved only the best, and he would see to it that she got it. She was *his* responsibility, and she was going to have a good life, he didn't care what he had to do to make it happen.

By the time Dominic was a senior in high school, he had reached his full height and weight.

He was powerfully built with broad shoulders, a washboard stomach, and long muscled legs. He would have excelled in the sports program at his high school, but there was never any time for frivolous activities like sports.

He had a few friends he occasionally went out with; but, for the most part, he was a loner. Instead, straight from class, he went to work.

Tony's Garage was on 125th Street, where he did everything from fixing radiators to pumping gas.

His shift ended at nine o'clock; and, by nine-thirty, he was home wolfing down a simple meal cooked by Jenny. She too, had no social life after school.

When she came home, laundry, cooking and cleaning greeted her. Later, when Dominic had finished his supper, they both did their homework on the scarred, Formica table, and then fell into their beds exhausted.

Neither one could count on their worthless father, who disappeared for months at a time. When he *did* come home, he spread misery and grief around like presents.

His mind was a wasteland. Deteriorated by liquor and hatred, he never had a kind word to say to either of his children. He conveniently forgot that it was Dominic's job that kept them in the dump where they lived, *and* put food on the table.

One thing did change, however. He never raised his hand to Dominic or Jenny again.

Joseph, being a coward by nature, instinctively knew that Dominic would have torn him apart if he tried.

So instead, he screwed with his mind and derived much pleasure from the pain that he could still cause.

Dominic's sighed wearily, there were other more pressing issues on his mind besides his scumbag of a father.

Lately, Jenny had been spending a lot of time away from home. That was unusual for her because they were so close, preferring to spend time with each other rather than outsiders.

She'd walk through the door humming a little tune with this big goofy smile on her face. He'd have to repeat things two or three times before she'd answer him because she was so distracted and day-dreamy.

Dominic shook his head. Since when had his sister become so mysterious?

He would bide his time and let her keep her secrets. It was just a matter of time before she told him anyway.

# Chapter Six

"Oh, baby, yes…you're so sweet," crooned Eric Robinson into the silky, fragrant hair of Jenny Lockwood.

They were at Van Cortlandt Park, seated in his red Mustang, with Journey on the tape deck completing the mood.

"Please, Jen…let me show you how much I love you."

Eric's marauding hands were slipping under her starched white blouse, trying to cop a feel.

"I don't know if we should be doing this," whispered Jenny, who was secretly thrilled by the sensations coursing through her body.

Eric Robinson was so handsome and popular. He went to Lincoln High, where all of the rich kids went.

He had it all, a good home where he had two loving parents, nice clothes, plenty of food and money, and most importantly, security.

All of those things were alien to her, with the exception of her mother and Dominic, whose love she could always count on.

Eric was like her white knight. He was so good-looking with his golden blond hair, sea green eyes, and beautiful body.

He represented everything she wished her life could be like. It was by chance that they had met.

The ancient Plymouth that Dominic had picked up for two hundred dollars had broken down for the millionth time.

Eric zoomed up beside her in his flashy red car and offered her a ride to the nearest gas station, where he immediately turned on the charm and managed to convince her to meet him at the McDonald's on University Avenue after school the next day.

They had been having these clandestine meetings ever since.

"Honey, you trust me, don't you? How can this be wrong when it feels so right?"

Eric knew how to bullshit with the best of them. He used the same tired lines on every girl he ever dated and screwed, and that was plenty.

"I'm so nervous," she hesitated, "I've never done it before. What if I get pregnant?"

*God,* she thought. Dominic would have a fit if he knew that she was going alone to a secluded place with a guy he'd never met, much less contemplating sleeping with him.

She hated keeping secrets from her brother, but he was so overprotective that he probably would have scared Eric off with his toughguy act, which *was* no act.

No, it was better this way. She was seventeen, practically an adult. She could handle her private life on her own.

"Jenny, look at me," Eric tipped his finger under her chin gently. "Whatever happens, we'll handle it together, right?" His sparkling smile was on full wattage as he blinked impossibly green eyes at her.

"Right now all I want to do is love you."

He went in for the kill, sliding his hand stealthily up her smooth, tan thighs to rest against the soft center of her. He snaked his tongue into her sweet-tasting mouth and plunged into its minty depths, at the same time, he slowly inched his fingers under the elastic of her bikini panties and plunged them through her downy hair.

White-hot passion streaked through her like mercury.

She arched her back and moaned softly, "Oh, Eric, I love you so much."

Eric suppressed a victorious smile.

Chicks.

They had to be the stupidest people on earth.

He undid the tiny pearl buttons one by one, exposing her luscious breasts. Her bra took seconds to dispose of, and he did it with the practiced ease of a true player.

He bent his head to suck lightly on the rosy nubs while his fingers parted the lips of her sex, delving deep inside her rhythmically, making love to her with his fingers.

Jenny thought that she would fly apart into a thousand pieces, the feeling was so exquisite. She was so glad that he was her first. Eric was right, this *felt* right. She loved him more than she thought was possible, and she wanted him desperately.

"Please make love to me," she sighed, her voice throbbing with emotion.

Eric guided her hand to the bulging fly of his 501s and groaned, "Baby, I thought you'd *never* ask."

# Chapter Seven

During the next couple of months, they met whenever possible, practically tearing their clothes off in their haste to touch, taste, and make love to one another.

Jenny knew she was on thin ice; her brother was starting to get suspicious about all of the time she was spending away from home. He wanted to know what she was doing and with whom.

She managed to put him off with one lame excuse after the next. It was clear that he wasn't buying it, but for now he was willing to give her space.

**\*\*\*\*\*\*\*\*\*\***

When her period was a couple of days late, she wasn't that worried. Her cycle varied from month to month. On the tenth day, Jenny was told by the sympathetic counselor at the clinic that she was in the very early stages of pregnancy.

She walked all the way home in total disbelief. Jenny entered the apartment; grateful that Dominic and her hated father were not home.

She was in shock, her face burning up and icy cold at the same time. *God, how could I have been so stupid?*

The one time Eric didn't use a condom, and she had to get pregnant. What could be the impossible odds of that happening?

She was pacing the floor, trying to keep the rising panic from engulfing her.

How on *earth* could she face Dominic? What was she going to say to him?

She knew that this would kill him right down to his soul. He had plans for the both of them to go to college, pursue their hopes and dreams, and finally, *finally* get away from their father.

Jenny was wringing her sweaty palms in distress. She knew that when he found out, he would demand to know who the father was. She became dry-mouthed with fear for Eric.

Eric!

"Oh my God," she whispered.

Dominic had a wild temper and right now she feared for Eric's very life. She slumped against the wall and slid down it in a defeated heap. She had to find Eric and tell him. He deserved to be told the truth. How would he take it?

She gradually started calming down. Eric loved her, he did. He was always so sweet and gentle. He would do the right thing by her and their baby. She knew in her heart that he'd ask her to marry him. Relief flooded through her like a wave.

*Whatever happens, Jenny, we'll take care of it together. I promise. I just can't wait any more, baby...all I want to do is make love to you.*

"I hope with all my heart that you meant it," she said aloud, her voice echoing through the empty room. She grabbed her coat and left the apartment with a soft smile on her lovely face.

**\*\*\*\*\*\*\*\*\***

"What the fuck do you *mean*, you're pregnant?" Eric glared at her and backhanded her brutally across her face.

"This is just fuckin' fantastic! How do I know that little bastard's mine, anyway? It could be *anybody's*."

His face was tight with rage. *This stupid bitch is trying to trap me!*

"Eric," Jenny's voice trembled uncontrollably, "of course the baby is yours. I *love* you, you're the only one I've been with...I *swear* it!"

She had tears running down her face, and her slender frame was visibly quaking. She forcibly tried to control herself, because Eric hadn't come alone.

Stretching languorously in the front seat was a bleached blonde in a low-cut sweater. She was watching the exchange avidly; a gloating, satisfied smile was on her overly made-up face.

"You don't *love* me at all!" Eric sneered, filled with contempt. "If you did, you wouldn't have been so fuckin' stupid and get knocked-up, now would you?"

The blonde's cruel laughter reverberated in the air. She twirled her hair around her finger and stared blankly at Jenny.

Jenny could not have felt more pain than if he had taken a gun and shot her in the heart. How could he think for *one* minute that she would let anyone else touch her? How could he refer to their baby as a bastard? She was devastated to see the hatred in his eyes.

"What am I supposed to *do*, Eric?" Jenny was on the verge of hysteria. The man that she loved was a terrifying stranger. She had no one else to turn to.

"That's *your* problem, not mine," he said in a bored tone. "You're more stupid than you look if you think I'm gonna play daddy. For all I know, that brat could be any one of ten different guys' kid."

"I never bought that virgin crap anyway. See, I've *driven* past that rat-hole you live in, and I *know* you're nothing but white trash trying to leech on to the first decent guy you could nail.

"All you *ever* were to me was an easy lay, baby...nothing more." He laughed like a smartass. "Hey, why don't you do the world a big favor and go kill yourself. Nobody'd miss you anyway. And don't even *think* about naming me the father of that mistake, because I'll deny it, and we all know who they'll believe, now *don't* we."

"Eric, come *on*," whined the blonde. "I'm getting bored."

Eric spun on his heel, hopped into his car, and roared off without once looking back.

The ground lurched sickeningly under Jenny's feet. She felt like one of those poor, dead animals that she had seen run down on the freeway; bleeding and violated.

Her knees buckled and she fell to the ground. Sobs wracked her body. What an utter fool she had been.

Eric never loved her at all. He used her without any regard for her feelings whatsoever.

Jenny staggered to her feet. There was no way that she could confide in her brother now. She couldn't bear the shame of it, or the disgust he would probably feel toward her.

She felt unclean; unworthy of the respect and love that Dominic showered upon her. He must never know how low she had sunk.

Jenny knew what she had to do.

# Chapter Eight

The dingy office was located in a sleazy, run-down part of the city. Climbing up the short flight of stairs, she saw rats scuttling in every dark corner. Unfazed, she entered the depressing room and took a seat on the rickety fold-out chair and waited for someone to help her.

A tall, unkempt man came through a side door and asked her how much money she had. Jenny took out her wallet and pulled out fifty dollars. It was their food money for the week; she wordlessly handed it over.

"That's all I have." Her voice was small and defeated.

"Git' in the next room and take off your clothes. You'll find what you need in there," he gestured with a jerk of his tobacco-stained thumb. "I'll be there in a minute."

"You *can't* be the doctor!" she exclaimed, horrified. "Uh…what I mean is that…you don't …you don't look like one," she trailed off lamely.

She was dismayed; the guy was dirty-looking, unshaven, and his eyes were a sickly yellow color. She could smell alcohol on his rancid breath and there was a slight tremor in his hands.

He looked around in mock amazement. "I don't see *anyone* else in the room, do you? And who'd expect for a lousy fifty bucks anyway? Marcus Welby?" he cracked with a ribald laugh.

"It's just that…I mean, usually doctors have their degrees hanging on the wall and stuff."

"Hey, looky here, missy. I've done this hundred times over, so if you want to get it done, you'll do as I say. Otherwise, get the hell out!"

She didn't want to get an abortion here, she didn't want to get an abortion at all, but she had no other options. She didn't have the four hundred dollars to have one done at the clinic in town. Plus, she had heard of a few girls that had their abortions here, if you could stand the filth.

"Okay, I haven't changed my mind. Straight through there?"

**********

As she lay shivering on the table, her hands went protectively over her flat stomach. "Oh, my darling baby," she whispered.

Tears trickled down the sides of her face, landing in her ears and making them itch.

More than anything, she wanted this child. But how could she raise it? They barely scraped by as it was. There was no money left over from their rent, except the pittance for food and clothing.

Dominic worked like a slave, and if he found out that she was pregnant he'd quit school and work any extra job that he could. There was no way she would carry the burden of destroying her brother's life. The door swung open and the "doctor" shuffled in, wearing a dirty white coat.

"Are we ready?" he asked flatly.

*No! Don't touch my baby!*

Aloud she whispered, "Yes, I'm ready."

*Chapter Nine*

Dominic let himself inside the apartment and called out for Jenny. He was thrilled to see no sign of his miserable father. Maybe if they were lucky, he was passed out somewhere.

"Jenny…hey," he tapped lightly on her door with a grin. "Let me in."

A muffled voice from the opposite side of the door said, "I'll be out in a while, Dominic. I'm kinda wiped out."

Immediately frowning, he hesitated. "Are you sure you're fine? You sound funny."

"I'm fine…. I'm just tired…that's all. If you're hungry, there's some macaroni and cheese in the fridge. All you have to do is heat it up. I'll be out in a little bit."

"Okay." Shrugging, he turned and made his way into the tiny kitchen.

As Dominic's footsteps receded, she let out a shaky sigh. She was in no shape to see her brother right now. She felt sick and feverish. Jenny peered under the blankets. Blood was beginning to seep through her nightgown.

The man said that bleeding was normal, but it was so bright and thick. Wearily, she laid her head back down onto the pillow and fell into a troubled doze.

She slept fitfully and awoke to the sound of angry voices.

Her father was home.

She hated him with everything she had inside her. All he did was cause heartache. She sat up and almost blacked-out from the pain. Sweat ran down her body in torrents.

"Dominic, help me," she croaked, surprised to hear how thin her voice sounded.

35

She staggered outside her door, and down the hallway, unaware of the blood running down her legs.

**\*\*\*\*\*\*\*\*\*\***

"You'll never amount to anything but what you are…and that's a fuckin' loser," said Joseph.

He belched sourly and glared at Dominic through bloodshot eyes. How he hated and envied his son. He belittled him every chance he could get. Never in a million years could he come close to being the responsible man that he had played no part in raising.

"Shut your stinkin' mouth, old man," warned Dominic. "Look at you. *You're* the one who's the loser. Why don't you do the world a favor and drop dead."

A slight whimpering noise caused Dominic to whirl around. The hairs on his arms and neck stood on end.

"Jesus *Christ*!" he exclaimed in stark terror.

He knocked over two chairs as he rushed to his sister. The front of her nightgown was covered from stomach to toe in blood. She looked terrible; there was a gray cast to her face and her pupils were dilated and unfocused.

He gently cradled her in his arms; the shock was reverberating through his trembling body like a currant. "What *happened*, Jenny? Did you get into some kind of accident? What's happened to you?" He barely kept a lid on his hysteria.

"Call an ambulance!" He bellowed to his father, who surprisingly did what he was told.

Dominic's mind was in disjointed turmoil. His sister was fine two hours ago. She hadn't left her room or he would have known.

"Jen, please tell me what's *happened*!" he said frantically.

He could barely speak through his tears. "Oh God, what happened to your face!" He softly touched the ugly purple bruise on her cheek.

Jenny knew that she was dying. It was fitting that Dominic's face was the last thing that she would see.

"He…he hit me."

Dominic saw white spots in front of his eyes. "Who *hit* you?" he asked in a tight, controlled voice. *Oh my God...this is not happening.*

"Please don't be ashamed of me when I tell you," she begged.

"I could never, *never* be ashamed of you, Jenny-penny."

The use of his childhood nickname for her made her smile. "I was pregnant up until three o'clock today. I really loved him Dominic...I did. But he didn't love me back, he only pretended."

She was struggling for breath. "He...he...said that the baby wasn't his, he called my child a bastard. He told me that I was low-class garbage. He...he...wished that I were dead. He wished that I would kill myself," she breathed.

"I was less than nothing to him, Dominic. Oh God, how could I have been so *stupid?*"

Tears were dripping off her chin, and rolling onto his hands. "I went to that place on Decatur Street, and...and I did it," she sobbed. "I killed my baby. Something must have gone wrong, because I'm dying Dominic...and I'm scared...I'm so *scared.*"

"Don't talk like that, baby, don't even *think* it," he said, panic-stricken. "I love you and I won't *let* you die. WHERE IN THE *HELL* IS THE AMBULANCE?" he screamed.

He turned back to Jenny and gently brushed her hair away from her forehead. "I want you to rest now. Help is on the way. You were so brave to have faced that all alone. You don't have to feel scared, because you're stuck with me, and I'm not going *anywhere.*"

He had never felt so helpless in his life. His sister meant everything to him, and to see her bleeding and broken in spirit was more than he could endure.

"Dominic, listen to me," Jenny laced her cold fingers through his, "you are the most extraordinary person I have ever known. I'm proud...to call you brother."

Every breath she took was an effort, but she was determined to speak these last words. "I don't want you to mourn me like you do Mama," she whispered. "I want you to have a happy life...full of exciting people and places. You deserve to be happy."

There was blood trickling out of the corner of her mouth and her grasp on Dominic's hand was loosening, "I'll always be inside you…"

**\*\*\*\*\*\*\*\*\*\***

Jennifer Lockwood died at 9:43 p.m., in the arms of the only person left in the world who had ever cared about her.

Dominic threw back his head and screamed in pain, rage and confusion. He rocked to and fro with his dead sister cradled to his chest.

The medical help, of course, came too late. As Joseph silently let them in, they looked on with sympathy at the tragic sight of the young man in unbelievable torment.

"Stay the *hell* away from her," he snarled, when they gently tried to wrest the dead girl out of his arms.

"Please sir," the EMT said, "you can follow us to the hospital, and someone will help you with the arrangements."

"I've buried my mother…I know what to do," he said dully, all of the fight drained out of him. "I'll meet you at the hospital."

## Chapter Ten

"She had massive internal bleeding, Mr. Lockwood. Whoever performed the abortion butchered her."

The overworked doctor had seen his share of senseless deaths, but it still angered him deeply. The poor girl would have lived, had she gone to a reputable clinic. It was a needless tragedy.

"I'm so very sorry that I couldn't save her."

"Thank you, doctor."

The shock was starting to wear off on Dominic and in its place was a cold, frightening fury. Jenny never had time to tell him the name of the bastard who used her like a whore and then trashed her soul.

He clenched his jaw and stalked through the hospital, unaware of the people scattering out of his way. He looked dangerous and vicious. Only his eyes betrayed the anguish that was in his heart.

If it were the last thing he would do, he would locate the monster that had violated his sister.

When he did…the fucker would wish he were *dead*.

But, first things first. There was one other person he had to deal with.

He smiled a deathly grin and headed towards Decatur Street.

**\*\*\*\*\*\*\*\*\*\***

Sheldon Leevy was counting up the totals for the day. Not bad, over two thousand buckeroonies. That was better than yesterday. He swigged from a half-empty bottle of Johnny Walker and belched loudly.

"Stupid, sluts all a ya..." he slurred drunkenly.

He owed his existence to those stupid girls who spread their legs and thought nothing of the consequences. They came, begging him to do away with their mistakes, pleading with him to help them. Of course, he would gladly do just that.

For a price.

He had been operating illegally for three years now. Eluding the law by a code of silence perpetuated by his victims, vulnerable girls with very little money and usually no one who really cared whether they lived or died.

There were many that had died at his hands, a fact that never once bothered Sheldon.

The loud kick of the office door snapped him out of his muse. The sight he beheld almost caused him to lose his bowels.

The man framed in the doorway was huge. Muscles bulged, as big as rocks on his long brawny arms, the rest of him looked just as muscular and intimidating. But it was his face that made Sheldon cringe in terror.

He had the face of a stone-cold killer.

His eyes were flat and cold, and his mouth was a tight, thin line. His mitt-sized hands were clenching and unclenching in to fists at his side, and his breathing was harsh and rapid. He had the blank, disconnected look of a maniac.

Sheldon cut his eyes to the tight white T-shirt he was wearing. He had dried blood smeared all over the front of it.

"Who *are* you?" he breathed. He forgot all about the money in his hand, it slipped through his fingers unnoticed.

The ominous man continued to stare at him, saying nothing. Only his eyes had changed. They were molten with hatred and malice.

He walked slowly towards Sheldon and stopped two feet in front of him. "Shut up," he whispered. His voice was a soft hiss.

Sheldon started to speak and never saw it coming. Dominic threw a punch and it landed with a sickening crack against the side of his jaw.

Sheldon fell back, over-turning a tray of dirty instruments. He groaned and tried to crawl away in vain.

Dominic stood over him and said, "I'm gonna do the talking."

He kicked him hard in the solar plexus and watched with enjoyment as the other man bellowed in pain.

Sheldon rolled on his side and threw up. The smell was nauseating.

"You performed an abortion on my only sister today. You must remember her, hmm?

"She was beautiful and innocent, and she came to *you*, you *fucking* piece of garbage," Dominic's eyes were red-rimmed and alive with hatred. "An *animal* that butchers young girls, for anything you can squeeze out of them."

He picked Sheldon up by the scruff of his neck and roughly threw him down in a dented metal chair.

Sheldon tried to speak, but it was in vain. His jaw dangled like a door with a busted hinge.

"Shut up!" Dominic screamed.

He was out of his mind with rage and pain that filled his soul completely. Any part of him that was tender and loving was obliterated, wiped out as if it had never existed. He was forever frozen inside.

"Do you believe in retribution? Do you believe as the bible says...an eye for an eye?"

The broken-down man on the chair was practically writhing in terror. His eyes were bugging out, and snot, along with blood, ran down his miserable face.

Dominic looked swiftly around the dirty, depressing room and located a scalpel. Picking it up, he saw a thin film of rust and dried blood on it. His stomach churned wildly. How many girls was this used on before his sister?

He brought the instrument within millimeters of Sheldon's ravaged face.

"Whaddaya say, asshole? Think I should cut your throat first? Or maybe your balls? Hey, I know...I'll cut 'em both."

"Ahh..." A guttural scream was all Sheldon could manage. He flinched and waited for the inevitable.

Dominic raised the scalpel and brought it swiftly down on the right side of the man's face.

Blood arced and splattered on the wall from the force of the slice. Sheldon's face was a mass of blood and gore on the right side.

"Please…" he gargled desperately, fearing his life was going to be taken slowly and excruciatingly.

Dominic raised the bloody scalpel again, hovering this time over Sheldon's throat.

"Did you show *one* shred of compassion or human kindness towards my sister?" he asked in a soft menacing tone. "Huh? You worthless, *sick* fuck!"

Dominic turned when he heard a sharp knock on the door.

Detective Nick Rossi had become a friend to Dominic five years ago, at St. Mary's Youth Center, where he volunteered his time one day a week.

He shot hoops with the neighborhood kids and was generally there to counsel, listen, and advise them whenever he could.

Nick became Dominic's mentor and friend. He came from a broken home as well, and could empathize with Dominic completely.

He was amazed at the kid's maturity and intellect. What touched him the most was Dominic's love for his little sister. He protected and sheltered her like a mother hen with its chick.

Jenny was a lovely, gentle girl. Now she was dead. A bright young life snuffed out, *way* too early. It was an abomination and the thought of it made Nick sick to his stomach.

"Jesus, Dominic. I'm glad I came when I did, or I'd be takin' a stiff to the morgue."

Sheldon made a pathetic attempt at escaping, only to be thrown back into his chair. Dominic stuck his face about an inch from Leevy's.

"Killing you is *way* too easy. I want you to suffer a long, *long* time for what you did to my sister. My friend here, is gonna see to it. Isn't that right, Nick?"

"Gonna be doin' some time," said Nick. His eyes were like chips of black ice.

Dominic laughed a devil's laugh, dark and sinister. "Man, oh man, Leevy. Your asshole is gonna be the size of a grapefruit. You'll be everybody's bitch, and that's a *fact*. And I for one, couldn't think of it happening to a sicker animal than yourself."

Dominic's eyes darkened, and he began squeezing his fingers around Leevy's scrawny neck.

Detective Rossi wisely intervened. He pried Dominic's fingers from around the screaming man's throat.

"You're under arrest, dirtbag. You have the right to remain silent, blah…blah…blah…."

He yanked Leevy up by his bony arm and cuffed him in a matter of seconds.

He turned to Dominic and said mildly, "You know, I'm gonna have to do some talkin' to explain why this asshole's face looks like it got caught in a shredder."

Dominic put a hand on Nick's shoulder. "I can't thank you enough for taking care of this," his voice trembled. "Jesus, Nick…Jenny…" He couldn't even say the words.

He was still in a state of total disbelief. It was inconceivable that Jenny was dead and never coming back.

Nick stared into his friend's eyes. Dominic looked like he'd aged a hundred years at that moment.

"I'm sorry, man. I'm *so* sorry," he said helplessly. "I loved her too. She's with the angels now." He cleared his throat as tears came to his eyes. "Look, don't worry about a thing. I'll see to it *personally* that this fucker gets sent up for a long time."

He slapped Dominic on the back and turned to Leevy. "Let's go, Leevy. I gotta waste *more* time now, and take you down to County so they can slap a Band-Aid on you. Believe me, I'd rather just kick your ass into the nearest pit and be *done* with it…" His voice trailed away as they made their way down the stairs.

Dominic stood in the empty room for a moment. His tears were blinding him.

He failed Jenny.

He *failed* her.

He should have broken down the door to her room. She didn't sound like herself. He *knew* that. If only he could have *seen* her. He would have immediately taken her to the hospital and none of this would have happened.

He took one last look at the squalid room, and left it with the door wide open.

**\*\*\*\*\*\*\*\*\*\***

Dominic entered the apartment and his knees nearly buckled. Jenny's blood was everywhere, in the kitchen and all along the hall leading to her room.

Like a sleepwalker, Dominic went straight by his father, who was passed out on the sofa, snoring without a care in the world, and stumbled to his room.

Methodically, he started pulling out shirts, pants, socks and underwear, placing them in a battered suitcase. He loaded all of his possessions in the Plymouth and started back up to the apartment.

He reverently gathered all of his sister's things and put them gently in to a cardboard box. His fingers traveled over her small bracelet with the tiny four-leaf clover on it and slipped it in his pocket.

He brought the silly stuffed cat pillow that he won for her at a long-ago carnival up to his nose and breathed in her smell. It was soft and powdery, like a baby.

Jenny's books, knickknacks and small Bible were all that he had left of her. Her clothes, he would arrange to have donated to the church.

He picked up the box and swiftly left the depressing apartment where he had both the worst childhood and the greatest loves of his life. A love he shared with his mother and sister.

As far as he was concerned, his lousy father was dead.

He hoped that the landlord kicked his ass out on the street. Joseph had freeloaded off of him for the last time. His last obligation was to bury Jenny, and when he did, he was gone.

He got into his car and drove off into the cold night.

# Chapter Eleven

In the years ahead, Dominic never looked back. He worked any job he could to eat and put a roof over his head. He went to night school and got his G.E.D. and immediately started taking college courses in business. Dominic was extremely intelligent, and made top grades.

He soon discovered an interest in the stock market. Money fascinated him. He read *The Wall Street Journal* religiously...it became his bible.

From that point on, Dominic knew what he wanted to do with his life.

He started little by little, saving a few dollars from his paychecks and buying shares in small, promising companies.

Over the next several years, he ate, drank, and breathed work. He kept selling his shares at the right time, and then reinvested his money into bigger companies and real estate.

He had an uncanny, instinctive knack for knowing the right businesses to invest in, because the stocks skyrocketed right along with his bank balance.

By the time Dominic was twenty-eight he made his first million, and he parlayed *that* into a huge fortune. He suddenly became a major player and people began taking him seriously.

The years flew by in a blur after that. He owned apartment buildings, a small but respected newspaper, and real estate. He also had his own investment company in Manhattan.

He was a workaholic. It was not uncommon for him to work until 1:00 or 2:00 a.m., only to be back at the office at six-thirty in the morning. His employees both liked and feared him, because he was a hard taskmaster, on himself as well as others.

He had boundless energy and ambition, as well as a shark's sense of self-preservation. He was tough and street smart, gaining the respect and admiration of his business colleagues.

Those who tried to cross him lived to regret it. He went after them with a ruthlessness that was staggering.

Nobody fucked with him.

No one could ever get close to him either. He froze them out with one look of his wintry gray eyes. His colleagues nicknamed him "The Ice-man" because he never showed any emotion whatsoever. He was a money making machine.

Women on the other hand, were never a problem. They fell around him like ninepins. There were many that tried to hook him into marriage, but failed miserably. Dominic was, for the most part, a loner. He trusted no one.

Underneath his hard exterior, the scars of his youth were forever with him. Dominic never forgot Jenny and what was done to her for one second.

It was a permanent fixture in the back of his mind, as was her four-leaf clover bracelet he carried like a talisman in his pocket. She was the reason he pushed on, never giving up, always striving to do better.

The fact that he never found out the name of the man that had impregnated Jenny and broke her heart festered inside of him until it was like a cancer.

He searched through all of his sister's belongings and could not find one thing mentioning *any* guy she was seeing, or let alone loved. Likewise, the few friends that Jenny had known knew nothing about her dating anyone.

He longed to be able to find the bastard. He dreamed of killing the faceless man a thousand times over. He prayed to God every night to avenge Jenny's death.

\*\*\*\*\*\*\*\*\*

On Dominic's thirty-fourth birthday, he got his wish. He was in his fabulous penthouse, replete with sex and the gourmet dinner that his date, a beautiful attorney, had prepared.

Davina was a tiger in bed. Dominic doubted he'd be able to walk straight for the rest of the night.

The lovely Davina departed in a cloud of Chanel and silk, with promises of a repeat performance.

He found himself alone and sitting on the polished hard wood floor in nothing but a pair of ancient 501s that fit his superb body like a glove.

In front of him was a small mahogany chest where Jenny's possessions reposed on a bed of midnight-blue velvet.

They were old friends, he reflected. They had seen him through his struggle to the top.

He ran his fingers over everything, seeing her gentle face. He absently picked up her stuffed cat pillow and rested his cheek against it. Turning it this way and that, he noticed a small horizontal tear running along the seam. Frowning, he brought it closer for inspection.

He saw a glint of silver amidst the stuffing. "Holy shit," he whispered in disbelief.

He raced to the kitchen and grabbed a small paring knife. Carefully, he slit the pillow and was shocked to find a diary amongst the fluff. The silver lock was what he'd seen shining.

Dominic thought he would have a heart attack, it was pounding so rapidly. With trembling fingers, he opened the small diary.

Suddenly transported back to his childhood, he smiled through the tears that were blinding him.

"Thank you for the birthday present, Jen," he whispered.

He flipped to the last few pages and his blood ran cold. Jenny had written this last entry a few weeks before she died.

*Dear diary,*
*I'm in love! His name is Eric Robinson and he goes to Lincoln High. He is so handsome and popular. He comes from a great home. Not poor, like Dominic and myself. He is the best lover in the whole*

*world and makes me feel beautiful. I'm really glad I saved my virginity because we love each other so much. That's the way it should be. Dominic doesn't know yet. I hate to keep it a secret from him, he's the best brother, and I love him very much. But Dominic is a worrywart, and I think for now it's best to keep it to myself. I want to introduce my two favorite guys, but the timing has to be right. I hope they become friends. I love them both. Gotta go!*

**\*\*\*\*\*\*\*\*\*\***

"I've *got* you," he whispered harshly.

He now knew the name of the man who, in effect, killed his sister. Tracking him down would be a piece of cake. His vast wealth assured him of that.

An evil smile spread across Dominic's face.

A seed of an idea began to germinate like a poisonous virus. Eric Robinson would have everything and everyone he cared about snatched away from him.

And *then,* he would pay…and *pay.*

# Chapter Twelve

**The Present**

Anna alighted from the low-slung sports car and nervously licked her lips. She and Dominic did not exchange one word on the drive to his country estate in the Hamptons. Instead, Sade was crooning about love being stronger than pride, in her rich, smoky voice.

She was glad for the music. What was she going to talk about anyway? The weather?

She turned her head towards the window and soaked in the glorious view, what little she could see of it anyway.

The sky was ink, with swollen bruised clouds hovering ominously. His mansion flanked the ocean. The property had lush flower gardens and thick, leafy trees abounded, ensuring total privacy.

The mansion itself was breathtaking. It was an elegant structure of glass, stone and whitewashed wood.

Anna could see tennis courts and a gazebo in the distance.

She guessed from his appearance that Lockwood was wealthy, but nothing on this grand scale.

Dominic quietly watched the myriad of emotions that flicked across her face. It was hard to believe that underneath that lovely exterior was a calculating gold-digger.

"Let's get inside, it looks like rain," he said abruptly.

Dominic opened the huge front door and held it for her. "Come on…it's okay." He spoke to her as he would an uneasy child.

Anna warily stepped inside, almost gasping at the simple beauty of her surroundings. The wood floors were the same cool whitewash color as the exterior outside, only polished to a glossy luster.

Exquisite rugs in mellow blue, creams and soft grays were casually thrown here and there. The walls were a soft eggshell color with paintings by Degas, Picasso and stark modern art blending together harmoniously.

The ceiling must have been thirty feet high with delicate freizes of soft clouds on a backdrop of pale blue sky. Anna continued walking as if she had no will of her own.

This heavenly place called to something deep inside her. Floor-to-ceiling windows dominated the entire household. In the daytime the view had to be spectacular.

Squashy leather couches in cream and dove gray co-existed peacefully with the handcrafted pale coffee tables and bookcases.

A newspaper was strewn across one coffee table, while a basketball snuggled up to a potted tree. The books in the bookcase were in no particular order and some were battered and dog-eared.

An ancient, fat tabby dozed on an exquisite footstool with no thought of its cost.

"Your home is lovely," she said quietly.

"Consider it your home…for now," he added.

The rough burr of his voice sent a shiver down her spine.

The whole situation was bizarre beyond comprehension. She certainly wasn't going to let him think she'd be comfortable here.

"But it's not *my* home…it's yours. We're total strangers, and I don't want to be here at all. I don't trust you. I don't know why you've brought me here or why you'd pay off my husband's debts.

"Speaking of which, Eric hasn't sent me any divorce papers that *I* know of, so why did you refer to him as my ex-husband?"

Dominic smiled slightly. "I don't know about you, but I'm starving. We have all the time in the world to answer your questions. You're not going anywhere."

Anna felt her heart leap, in spite of herself, "Are you keeping me here against my will?"

"I don't have to. You made your choice by coming with me. Now that you *are* here, you're staying. I wouldn't have it any other way," he added with a dangerous smile.

\*\*\*\*\*\*\*\*\*

The dining room was just as elegant as the rest of the house. Heavy sterling silverware rested next to fine bone china so thin it didn't seem like it could support the weight of a dinner roll.

Waterford flutes containing perfectly chilled champagne sparkled against the candlelight. Fresh roses and gardenias beaded with dew reposed in a priceless crystal bowl.

They dined on fresh Maine lobsters, asparagus, and fluffy rice pilaf. It was cooked to perfection. They both ate in silence.

Anna was so nervous that she barely touched her plate. Dominic ate with an enormous appetite, enjoying every bite of his meal.

She assumed he had some kind of housekeeper, but she hadn't seen a soul yet. The food was already on the sideboard when they entered the dining room. She struggled for something to say to break the uncomfortable silence.

"Are we alone here?"

"No. I employ an older couple. They live here on the grounds. I also have a full staff, but they go home at night. You'll like the Porters, especially Mrs. Porter," he smiled. "That woman makes the best pies I've ever tasted. They're both good people."

Dominic's eyes were soft as he spoke of the couple. It was very apparent that he was fond of them. The transformation was amazing. His mouth was almost vulnerable, and his eyes shimmered like quicksilver.

"Do you have any family living here?"

Anna quailed at the abrupt change in Dominic's expression. Gone was the almost human dinner companion. In its place was the hard, cold stranger who terrified her earlier.

"I have no family."

The flat, toneless way he spoke was frightening. The moment was uncomfortable and strained. Anna twisted her hands together and said nothing.

"If you'll excuse me, I have some business calls to make. You can have coffee and dessert in your suite if you want. I'm sure you're probably tired. Goodnight, Anna." He scraped back his chair and rose from his seat.

"Please wait."

She jumped out of her chair at the same moment he did. "I'm sorry...I didn't mean to pry. It was an innocent question, really."

Anna was getting more confused by the minute. This man's moods were impossible to gauge. One minute he was almost approachable, the next he was menacing.

She was starting to think she made the wrong choice coming here. Anna quickly banished the unwelcome thought from her mind. She shuddered. She was lucky she didn't end up in Johnny's clutches.

But what did Lockwood *want* from her? That was the million-dollar question. She hoped fervently that he didn't *really* expect sex in lieu of payment.

He didn't seem like the kind of man that had to pay for his women. She was sure the opposite was true. He probably had to beat them off with a stick.

He was extremely handsome. His exotic, stylish persona was mesmerizing, so she had a hard time believing that it was a sexual reason that prompted his actions.

No...he had a hidden agenda, and she had to find out what it was.

His eyes softened a tiny fraction at her confusion. "You weren't prying. I really *do* have a lot of business calls to make, most of them are overseas."

He turned to the wall and pulled a velvet rope. "Someone will be up to draw your bath and show you around. The view from your suite is beautiful. Your dessert will be served to you whenever you wish."

He looked like he was going to say something else, but at the last minute changed his mind. "Goodnight."

He turned and walked out of the room leaving Anna trembling with a mixed bag of emotions. One thing was obvious. She was being dismissed. He probably didn't want her wandering around his private domain, she thought sourly.

"Excuse me, Mrs. Robinson?" The soft sound of a female voice jolted Anna out of her unhappy thoughts.

A young girl, perhaps fifteen or so, suddenly appeared. "Mr. Lockwood wants me to show you to your room. It's right this way."

# *Chapter Thirteen*

Anna entered the suite and sighed softly. She had never been in such a lovely bedroom.

The room was huge and airy. The wood floor beneath her feet was buffed to a high polish. It was softened with fluffy lamb's wool throw rugs in subtle cream colors.

The king-size bed was decadent. It was a four-poster made from pale wood with beaten silver and Lapis Lazuli inlaid on the massive headboard. Filmy white chiffon formed a delicate curtain around the bed. Anna separated the curtain and spied fat goose down pillows piled high; they looked so soft and inviting.

The enchanted bed charmed her. It was like something out of an *Arabian Nights* story. The dresser, vanity and night tables also were inlaid to match the bed. A huge granite fireplace was ablaze with fragrant driftwood.

Big, squashy pillows in burgundy were thrown casually against the cream suede couch and loveseat. Silken curtains were open to the sea, now dark and angry sounding.

Shivering slightly, she followed the teenager into the next room.

Anna let out a low whistle. The bathroom was all marble, glass and granite. The massive sunken tub was big enough for four people to bathe in. Thick, scented candles flickered, their flames dancing as she gazed in wonder at the opulence surrounding her. This kind of luxury was completely foreign to her.

Soft bath sheets rested on a heated towel rack, and bath crystals in every color of the rainbow glittered like diamonds on the ledge of the tub.

Lucy Porter smiled, understanding. "I know what you mean. If they had bathrooms like this at school, I'd never leave."

Anna smiled back, liking the young girl instantly. "Do you go to school around here?"

"Nope. I'm just here visiting my grandparents for winter break. I go to boarding school in Pennsylvania. My parents are on kinda a second honeymoon, so here I am. By the way, my name is Lucy Porter," she added with a charming grin.

"Of course. You're the granddaughter of the caretakers," Anna hesitated, "I don't know their first names."

"William and Katherine," Lucy said affectionately.

"You sound like you really love them." Anna was wistful. She had never known either set of her grandparents. They'd died before she was born.

"Oh, I do," Lucy said, as she began to turn on the bath taps. She sprinkled a healthy amount of bath crystals into the tub.

"They're, like, so totally cool. Gramma always knows when I'm bummed out, and she gives the best advice. Plus, I gain about a pound on all the goodies she makes!"

Anna laughed, "I heard that her pies win awards."

"Man, do they ever! Her chocolate cream pie is amazing."

"Well, it sounds heavenly."

"Gramps is great too, he's, like...*so* easy to talk to."

Lucy gestured for her to get into the tub, which was now a mass of twinkling, sweet-smelling bubbles. It seemed she was going to get the royal treatment. Oh well, after the day *she* had, Anna certainly wasn't going to argue.

Gratefully, she peeled off her clothes and sank into sheer bliss as the warm water swirled around her like a cocoon. She groaned in spite of herself, "God, this feels good."

Lucy giggled, "I can tell. You just lay back and enjoy. I'll be outside turning down your bed. Yell when you want your hair washed, okay?"

"Okay."

Anna settled down amongst the iridescent bubbles and ruminated about the day's events. Picking up a cake of French milled soap, she absently washed herself, only half aware of the sensuous feel of the slippery smooth bar as she slid it up her slender arms and down her legs.

She only now realized that Dominic neatly avoided answering any of her questions. It was as if he deliberately sidetracked her. She frowned. Well, maybe it wasn't on purpose. After all, he did seem genuinely distressed when she asked about his family.

How was *she* supposed know that it was such a sore subject? Tomorrow she would demand to know just what in the hell was going on. Minutes passed as Anna luxuriated in the soothing water. A soft tap on the door signaled Lucy. Anna had her eyes closed.

"Come on in, Lucy." she sighed tiredly. "I can't remember the last time I had my hair washed for me!"

Eyes still closed; she lay back in the tub and prepared to be pampered. Gentle fingertips worked the shampoo through her hair in circular motions, then a draught of warm, clear water cascaded over her head to rinse away the suds, only to have the same hypnotic procedure repeated again.

This time the long fingers were slow and sensuous as they wove themselves through the wet, black silk. Anna's heart began to pound. *No! It can't be. Don't be ridiculous!*

Of course it was Lucy! She was exhausted and her mind was playing tricks on her. The hands continued their downward exploration of her creamy neck and shoulders, massaging all the tension out of her.

Another kind of tension was building up inside her. The hands were very strong and large. Not the hands of a young girl. She still did not open her eyes. If they were closed, she could pretend she didn't know who it was.

The callused palms paused against her breast to feel the thunder of her heartbeat.

Anna lay dry-mouthed and spellbound, powerless to lift a finger. The big hands covered her breasts for a breathless moment, and then it was over.

Anna gasped as a cascade of cool water streamed over her head.

By the time she got the water out of her eyes, the room was empty. She looked around swiftly. That was impossible. Only a few seconds had passed.

"Lucy?"

She quickly wrapped a warm bath sheet around her and went running into the bedroom. Lucy was just coming through the bedroom door.

"Oh! I thought you'd still be in the bath. I brought your purse from downstairs. I don't know about you, but I can't stand to be without mine." She laid it on the dresser.

Anna was trying to get her heartbeat under control. "Thank you, Lucy," she managed to squeak. "Um," she licked her lips nervously, "did you happen to see Mr. Lockwood in here? I mean...did you pass by him?"

Lucy looked at her strangely, "No, I'm sorry. I didn't. Would you like me to get him for you?"

She was almost out the door before Anna cried out. "No! I don't want to disturb him. I'll just talk to him in the morning."

"All right. Well, is there anything else I can get for you? Some dessert or coffee?"

"No, Lucy, thanks. You've been great. I think I'll just turn in."

"Goodnight, Mrs. Robinson."

"Goodnight."

She was finally alone.

She looked out at the ocean, visible only when the forked lightening illuminated it eerily. She was in the home of a cold, foreboding stranger, and there wasn't a damn thing she could do about it.

## Chapter Fourteen

The storm had hit with a vengeance. The thunder sounded like something out of an old Vincent Price movie, and the rain was pelting the window like machine-gun fire.

Anna wandered throughout the room, pausing here and there to pick up small knickknacks. She was unaware of how erotic she looked with her pearly white skin and tangled hair framing her face like an ebony lion's mane.

She walked to the huge closet and opened it. She gasped softly, and touched her hand to her throat. *No, it couldn't be.*

It was filled with expensive, designer clothes. Anna reached out and reverently touched a black satin gown.

There were racks of shoes in every color and style, as well as purses and accessories. The vanity held an untold treasure trove of cosmetics. The best Lancôme had to offer.

She lifted a crystal stopper to her nose and breathed in the heavenly scent of Chanel No.5. She touched the slender glass tube against her neck, jumping slightly at the cool touch of the stopper.

Shivering, Anna went to the tall armoire and opened it, hoping to find something to sleep in. The pungent fragrance of potpourri wafted through the air as Anna gazed wide eyed at the most exquisite lingerie she had ever seen.

It was like a box of chocolates, where the next candy was more sumptuous than the last. She pulled out a pair of pajamas in heavy cream-colored satin. The style harked back to the 40s. It had a severe masculine cut that made the wearer look more feminine than if she were in frills and lace.

Anna sat in front of the fire and brushed her hair until it fell in silky ribbons down her back.

He had planned on her being here all along. It was a disturbing fact.

All the beautiful clothes and cosmetics were purchased exclusively for her. The room, everything, seemed to be waiting for her to occupy it. She nervously chewed her bottom lip. She was here for a very specific reason, and she desperately wanted to know what that reason was.

She kept going over the bizarre scene in the bathroom. How dare he go in there uninvited and...and...cop a cheap feel!

She was disgusted. *Hypocrite! You enjoyed it. You know you did.*

"Shut up!" She muttered aloud to her stupid conscience. She was ashamed and sickened by her reaction.

So what if he looks like a Greek God? Sometimes dangerous things came in sleek, sexy packages.

A vague sense of unease crawled down her spine. Why would he spend a huge fortune on someone he obviously despised?

She caught him staring at her at dinner and the look in his eyes could only be described as...well...hatred. He had some how gotten it into his head that she knew about the incredible amount of money Eric had stolen from him. He treated her with barely disguised contempt.

Anna didn't think for one minute that she could just walk out and leave now. He *meant* for her to stay. He said so himself. She couldn't fight him even if she wanted to. He could overpower her in an instant, couldn't he?

He had gotten physical with her already, back at her place. He could just as easily do it again. A huge flash of lightening and rolling thunder ripped through the air. Anna jumped to her feet in fright as the electricity went dead.

Her heart was thumping so hard she could barely stand. Anna's imagination went into overdrive, and took a turn for the worse as the storm increased in its fury.

What if Dominic had lied to her? Maybe Eric *didn't* leave of his own accord. Dominic was a hard, intimidating man, both physically and mentally. No match for her husband. Or her ex-husband.

*Or your dead husband.*

Anna pressed her hand hard against her mouth. No matter how much she tried, she couldn't keep the paranoid thoughts at bay.

*Stop it!* her mind commanded.

Just how much *did* she know about Dominic Lockwood anyway? Exactly nothing.

Just because he was seriously rich didn't mean he was a nice guy. Hell, he *wasn't* a nice guy. He was cold and remote.

No one knew where she was, or even cared, for that matter. Anything could happen to her and no one would ever know. She walked to the huge glass window and peered into the darkness.

The landscape was lonely and deserted. She couldn't see a thing except for the waves breaking violently against the beach. She leaned her forehead against the cold glass and tried unsuccessfully to calm down.

"It's just the storm," she whispered.

If he'd wanted to do her any harm, he could have already done it.

*Yes, but what if he wants to have a little fun with you first? He could rape, torture, and kill you for his own pleasure, and no one would ever know about it.*

She moaned aloud. *You're being an idiot, Anna! Just stop it.*

A neon flash of lightening lit up the beach, and Anna gasped in fright. Dominic was outside on a huge black stallion. He had on black rain gear with a Stetson pulled low over his face. He was silently looking up at her through the glass. A second later, the sky was pitch black again.

She stood shaking like a leaf; cold sweat trickled between her breasts. The next instant, the sky was again illuminated. The beach was windswept and deserted. There was no trace of him. How could he have disappeared so fast? Was she going crazy? Everything at the moment seemed so surreal.

Anna streaked towards the bed and dove in between the covers like a coward. He was there, dammit! She saw him.

He looked…scary. What was he *doing* out there?

She lay awake for the longest time and finally drifted off into a troubled sleep. She woke up once in the middle of the night. Disorientated, she groped her way to the door and turned the cool brass knob. It wouldn't budge. She was locked in.

She made her way back to the bed and stared at the filmy chiffon curtain surrounding her.

*Please let me be dreaming.*

Sleep finally calmed her at quarter after four.

## Chapter Fifteen

Anna rose with a jolt at nine o'clock and scrambled out of bed. She ran to the door and tried the knob. It turned smoothly, and the door opened out into the plush hallway.

"Good morning, Anna." Dominic seemed to materialize out of thin air.

"Oh!" she jumped, "you startled me."

He smiled slightly, "I'm sorry, you looked a little lost. I didn't mean to startle you."

"That's okay," she mumbled.

Well, he certainly didn't *look* like the sinister being she saw last night. In fact, quite the opposite was true.

The coal black turtleneck and linen slacks he wore looked great on him. His long hair hung perfectly from a center part, and brushed softly past his shoulders. He looked big, masculine, and heart-stoppingly handsome.

"Are you hungry?" he inquired politely.

To her surprise, she was. "Yes, I am."

"Good. We'll have breakfast in the atrium."

"Okay." She looked down at her tousled self. "If you can give me a minute," she said self-consciously.

"No." His eyes penetrated her own. "Please...stay as you are," he said quietly.

Anna could feel herself falling under his spell. His charm was deadly.

"All right, lead the way."

She decided to go with the flow. To fight him in his own home would be useless. They walked together in companionable silence down airy hallways illuminated by the huge skylights above.

They entered the atrium and Anna turned to Dominic, astonished. "It's so lovely," she gasped. "I've never seen anything like it."

She was at a loss for words. She walked as if in a trance.

The atrium was immense. It's domed roof towered above them. All the walls were made entirely of thick plated glass. The ocean, glorious and majestic, stretched on as far as the eye could see, in all three directions.

Tall, flowering trees grew in lavish abundance. White roses and gardenias made the air intoxicating. Ferns, frangipani, and orchids were everywhere. The air was soft, moist, and warm.

There was even a small pond with lotus blossoms and lily pads. She peered closely and to her delight saw Koi fish swimming lazily, their white and orange colors shimmering in the water.

The pathway was smooth teakwood that rounded out into a huge circle in the center of the atrium. In the circle was a table set for two. It was magical. They were in the very heart of the foliage and flowers; and yet, the sea, still dark and turbulent, was a dramatic backdrop against the faint flashes of lightening and pouring rain still beating at the glass.

Dominic held her chair out for her and Anna sat down, smiling in wide-eyed wonder at this indescribably beautiful oasis.

Dominic settled back and asked her if she cared for coffee or juice. After pouring both of them cups of rich, fragrant coffee, Anna decided to take the bull by the horns.

"Where is my husband, Mr. Lockwood? And how come you seem to think he's my ex-husband?"

"I've no idea where Eric is, and I don't care, but I *do* have proof that he's no longer your husband."

Dominic pulled out a manila envelope from the bottom rack of the food service and laid it on the table in front of her. His face was expressionless.

Anna slowly opened the envelope and read the document. It was indeed a divorce decree from the Dominican Republic. As she read on, there was no doubt of its authenticity.

Anna looked up. "What if I don't want the divorce? What then?"

Dominic looked at her through hard gray eyes. "It's too late for second chances, Anna. Besides, why would you want to be hooked up again with that loser?"

She flushed under his iron gaze. "That's none of your business," she snapped.

"Correction," he stated flatly. "Everything you do from now on *is* my business. I suggest you stop and think about that. You're in *my* home and you're under *my* care and protection. *That* entitles me. Do I make myself clear?"

They locked eyes for several seconds. It rankled that she had to take orders from him. Anna knew her downfall was pride, and she didn't like being told what to do, especially by a virtual stranger.

*A virtual stranger who has total control of your life at the moment.*

She surrendered and dropped her eyes first.

"Crystal clear, *Mr.* Lockwood," she sneered.

Dominic took the document wordlessly, as if answering her snotty reply was beneath his dignity. He leaned back and folded his powerful arms in front of him. He stared dourly at her.

"How exactly are you and my husb…Eric, acquainted and why?"

"As if you *didn't* know."

"Hey…I *don't* know! Stop avoiding the subject and answer me!"

"Is this gonna be an inquisition, Miz Price? If so, tell me now, and I'll have my attorney present," he rapped out.

Anna gripped the sides of the table. He deliberately used her maiden name to rattle her, and it worked.

"How did you know my maiden name?"

"I know *everything* about you Anna, every ugly detail. Never forget that."

"Oh yes, how stupid of me." Anna could feel her temper reaching a boiling point. "I guess when you have an obscene amount of money you can afford the very *best* spies. And while we're on the subject of spying, how *dare* you barge in and…and *assault* me while I was bathing last night! I have a right to some privacy.

"Next time, try knocking, or better yet, why don't you just send one of your slaves to come get me!" She stopped her tirade long enough to catch her trembling breath.

"*Well?* Are you going to say something or not?" She yelled in a banshee-like voice, losing her cool completely.

A slow, lazy grin spread across Dominic's face. "My, my, what a *nasty* temper you have. I'm surprised the walls didn't crack."

Anna was mortified by her lack of self-control.

Look at him! He was enjoying her embarrassment thoroughly. She wanted to slap that sarcastic grin off his face. Instead, she took a deep breath and took a different tack.

"Look, I shouldn't have lost my temper like that, but all I want is some answers. Please…"

"I have every intention of answering your questions."

Dominic began calmly serving them ripe strawberries and melon into crystal bowls.

"I met Eric through an associate of mine. I hired him to do some freelance work for me. Obviously Eric wasn't into communication or you'd have known that, or maybe you do and you're just trying to see how much *I* know." He looked hard at her.

Anna flushed and was the first to look away.

"He stole quarter of a million bucks from me. He got caught and was given a choice. Stay and pay the consequences, or cut his losses and run.

"He chose the latter, Anna. He wrote you off without a second thought. But not before he told me that you were the brains behind everything. He pretty much blamed you for it all."

Anna sat in stunned silence. She knew Eric to be duplicitous and cowardly, but this was too much.

To actually lie, and lay the blame on her shoulders for something she was completely innocent of was unforgivable. She swallowed hard and spoke. "Why wouldn't you just turn him over to the authorities? Why give him any choice in the matter at all?"

Something strange and frightening flickered in Dominic's eyes. It came and went so fast she thought that she'd imagined it.

"That's not how I chose to deal with the situation."

"So why am *I* here, Dominic? If you think I'm guilty of some crime then why don't you have me arrested?"

He stared at her intently. "That's the first time you've called me by my name."

His voice was like a subtle caress. She couldn't think straight when he looked at her like that. She was painfully aware of her burning cheeks and prayed that he didn't notice.

"Don't change the subject. This is completely *insane*! You can't keep me here and expect me to act like it's the most normal thing in the world. It doesn't make any sense."

"Do you *want* to go to prison?" he asked derisively.

"No, of course not, but…"

"Let's just say that you serve a very important purpose and leave it at that."

He rose gracefully from the table and wiped his mouth with a snowy linen napkin. "Please stay and finish your breakfast, I usually just have coffee. I'll see you tonight."

"Hold it! You can't just take *off*! What'll I do all day?"

He looked at her enigmatically. "I'm sorry, but it can't be helped."

Dominic brushed a raven lock behind Anna's ear. "Mrs. Porter will be along any time and she'll take care of you. You're free to explore this house and grounds."

He glanced at his watch. "Oh, and Anna…? Before I forget, in defense of my actions last night. I *did* knock."

His gray eyes were shimmering with undisguised amusement. "You just assumed it was Lucy. When you asked for your hair to be washed, well…how could I *possibly* refuse such a tempting offer?"

He ran his finger softly down her jaw, turned, and strode out of the atrium. The beautiful room seemed less so without Dominic's magnetic presence.

Anna sighed and stood up. She wasn't hungry anymore. She walked up to the glass walls. The gunmetal gray sky was dark and ominous. The rain relentlessly pelted against the window. It matched her mood perfectly.

Dominic still managed to get away without answering her

questions to her satisfaction. If anything, she felt even more confused by his cryptic answers.

*How in the world have I come to this point?*

# *Chapter Sixteen*

**The Past**
**Northern California**

Anna Price was born in a small town in Northern California. She and her mother lived in a two-bedroom condo in a nice part of town.

Her parents divorced when she was only four years old, and her father never bothered to keep in touch with her. Her mother had to work two jobs to make ends meet.

Dorothy Price worked all day at the local supermarket, only to come home, cook a fast dinner for the both of them, and head out to clean offices at night. Weekends were the only real time she and her daughter had to spend together.

Dorothy wanted her only child to have a better life than she did. She encouraged Anna to study and keep her grades up. She had all the time in the world to get married and have babies. Dorothy wanted her to enjoy her youth.

Anna graduated with honors and was awarded a small scholarship of five thousand dollars. She enrolled in a junior college, and life went on as usual.

One night, Anna and her friend Debbie were cruising along in her old Civic when a bunch of guys with Litchfield College jackets pulled up alongside of them at a light.

The older one was the best looking of the bunch. Mr. Wonderful sat proudly behind the wheel of a bright red Mustang. He took one look at Anna and did the classic double take.

"Hey, beautiful…wanna party?"

Anna giggled, "What'd you have in mind?"

"I'm hosting a little frat party, and you two are the best lookin' babes I've seen all night. So, whaddaya say? You ladies interested?"

Anna grinned at her friend and shrugged. Aloud she said, "All right, lead the way."

**********

The music was deafening in the smoky frat house. Anna weaved her way through the throng of drunken football players and their equally drunken dates, and followed her blonde escort upstairs. The noise was marginally quieter in the cramped room.

"These parties get a little out of control, but there's nothing to worry about. You're safe with me."

Anna stood in the center of the room awkwardly. "I really should go see where Debbie has gone."

"Hey, pretty lady, your friend's fine with Steve. They're probably havin' a few brews and gettin' to know each other. Like we are."

She laughed a little. "I don't even know your name."

"My name's Eric Robinson. Pleased to meetcha." He grinned disarmingly and held his hand out.

Anna reached out and shook his hand. "Hi, I'm Anna Price," she said shyly.

"Know what? You're awful cute, Anna. You don't go here do you? I'd remember if you did."

"No. I go to a J.C. in Fair Oaks."

Eric held her stare and took a long swallow of beer. He set it down decisively on the nightstand and narrowed his eyes slightly.

This one was a knockout. He would have to have been both blind and stupid not to see all the guys checking her out as they passed by.

Her faded jeans hugged her slender body in all of the right places. Places that Eric wanted to pillage and plunder for himself. Her breasts were high and full, and the forest green turtle neck she wore was hornier than all the tits that were on display downstairs.

As far as Eric was concerned, it was her face that was the best of all. Electric blue eyes scorched him like a flame, and her mouth was what wet dreams were made of.

Her silky black hair was so soft looking and shiny, he wanted to run his fingers through it. Have her brush it all over his body.

Eric turned on his stereo, and as luck would have it, Chicago was on, slow and dreamy. "Let's dance," he said softly.

Anna felt a jolt from the top of her head to the soles of her feet. He was the best looking guy she'd ever seen. "Okay."

He wrapped his arms around her and they moved in a slow circle around the tiny room. Eric was getting a massive hard-on, and it was becoming difficult to hide. He began to subtly inch them in the direction of the bed.

"Mmm…you smell so good," he whispered in her ear.

Anna buried her head against his shoulder. "Thanks." She felt tongue-tied and shy.

She struggled to make conversation. "What are you majoring in?"

"Dunno yet. I don't have to worry about a major anyway, I'm fer sure gonna get a deal to play pro ball."

"*Wow*, really? What position do you play?"

Eric flexed a little. "Quarterback, of course. I'm surprised you haven't read *all* about me."

She smiled at him and lifted a brow. "I really never *read* the sports page."

Eric smiled back sheepishly. "Oh yeah…right. Well anyway, I'm expecting a visit from a scout for the Forty-Niners any day now."

Anna was impressed and more than a little flattered. He could have had his pick of any girl and he chose *her*.

Eric, on the other hand, was trying to figure out how he was going to get this luscious little piece into the sack. He pulled her closer, sliding his hands over her butt.

"Let's get more comfortable." He eased her gently down onto the unmade bed in one fluid movement.

"Hey, wait just a *minute*!" Anna shot off of the bed like a rocket and whirled around.

"If you think you're gonna get some cheap piece of tail you can *damn* well think again!"

Eric was flabbergasted. He assumed that she wanted it too. No chick had ever turned *him* down before.

"Relax, baby, I didn't mean no harm."

His hands were turned up in a gesture of innocent bewilderment.

Anna wasn't buying it. She was pissed off. He needed to know right up-front that she wasn't some dumb little bimbo.

"Don't call me baby! I have a name, so *use* it. Another thing, I don't even *know* you yet. Did you honestly think that I was going to *sleep* with you?"

It sounded like a great idea to Eric, but he had to admit that she was a nice change from all the girls around campus.

It was a refreshing change.

Besides, she looked totally hot with her eyes shooting angry sparks at him. In fact, her anger was beginning to turn him on. He thought he could spot an erect nipple through her sweater, but didn't want to stare.

"Look, Anna…I apologize, truly I do. I was out of line *totally*. It'll never happen again. That is, if you don't want it to." He added hopefully.

Anna relaxed and even managed to laugh a little. "Okay. I'm sorry too. I didn't mean to bite your head off. Why don't we go find Debbie and Steve."

Eric smiled ruefully. He *had* to respect the girl.

## Chapter Seventeen

The months flew by in a blur for Anna. She and Eric had been together since that fateful night. Their relationship was up and down. Anna loved him, but it was getting harder and harder to trust him.

There were many times she had caught him in lies. She also knew he had cheated on her before because one of her friends said she'd seen him all over some girl at a party.

Eric was *always* sorry afterwards. He came back begging her to forgive him. It was the same, time after time.

He would have tears in his eyes, proclaiming his utter love and devotion to her. He knew all the right buttons to push, because sooner or later Anna would give in and things would be great, until the next time.

Dorothy Price privately thought her daughter's beau was a conceited, arrogant jerk. She recognized his type a mile away. All flash, and no class or integrity whatsoever.

Oh sure, he was good-looking, a fact which he used shamelessly to his advantage. He also knew how to turn on the flattery and charm, but it was surface only. He was about as deep as a thimble and a liar too.

Dorothy knew better than to voice her opinions to her headstrong daughter. That was the quickest way to drive her even further into his lying, cheating arms. Dorothy hoped that Anna would wise up and drop him like a bad habit. Until then, she could only dream.

**\*\*\*\*\*\*\*\*\***

Dean Henry Pruitt took off his reading glasses and said grimly,

"Come in, Mr. Robinson, and close the door. Coach Lipton will be here shortly. Ah, good…here he is right now. Afternoon, Chuck."

Chuck Lipton came in just behind his star QB. "Afternoon, Dean."

Lipton had been dreading this meeting all morning long. He walked into the large office and sat to the right of Dean Pruitt.

"Have a seat, Mr. Robinson."

Eric's eyes shifted from the Dean to Coach Lipton. He felt a sudden sense of foreboding. Whatever this was about, he, Eric Robinson, was about to get shit on.

Henry Pruitt leaned forward and opened a file. "It's come to my attention that you've been dealing and using drugs."

"Wait! I can explain, Dean."

"Don't *ever* interrupt me, Mr. Robinson. Is that clear?"

"Yessir," he mumbled.

This was really bad. Eric felt a violent case of diarrhea coming on.

Pruitt continued, "Please do not *insult* my intelligence. Three other athletes have already been caught, and all three name *you* as the leader of their pack."

Eric grasped at straws. "They're lyin', Dean! I swear it! Ya gotta believe me! Coach…? *Say* something! You *know* I'd never do that."

Lipton shook his head sadly. "I wish I could, son. But we both know that it wouldn't be the truth."

Eric wanted to kill his so-called friends. He never would have ratted on his buddies! Those scummy bastards deserved to get the *crap* kicked outta them.

Dean Pruitt disliked liars, but he especially hated bad liars. He decided to put Robinson out of his misery. He pulled out an 8 x 10 glossy of Eric exchanging money for drugs with Benny Salvatore, a well-known coke dealer in town.

"Pictures don't lie, do they, Robinson? If this were the only smear on your record, I *might* have overlooked it. Unfortunately, that's not the case. You've been caught cheating on tests numerous times, and your teachers complain about your disruptive behavior in class constantly.

"The police bust up the drunken soirées at the frat house on a regular basis. They see more of you than your own *parents* do! No more. Enough is enough!

"I've *had it* with all of you jocks getting preferential treatment. As of twelve noon tomorrow you're expelled from Litchfield *permanently*. I've already informed your parents of your expulsion. I'm sure they'll be contacting you today."

Eric's jaw hung open in disbelief. His world was crumbling around his feet. He looked to Coach Lipton for salvation, but *he* just stared down at the wood grain of Pruitt's desk, as if all of life's mysteries were written upon it.

"What about my shot with the 'Niners? I'm still the best damn quarterback this school has ever seen!"

Lipton looked up and cleared his throat. "Sorry, Eric. No decent scout is gonna touch you now. This can't be swept under the rug. Dealing drugs blew any chances of you playing with the pros. Not to mention you doing them. You've got a big cocaine habit."

Eric sucked in his breath painfully. He was close to tears. "Please," he said desperately. "Give me another chance. I swear I'll bring my grades up and I'll never do coke again, *ever*. *Please* don't kick me out."

Dean Pruitt had his mind made up. "Save it, Robinson. My mind *cannot* be changed. You're excused."

"Well, FUCK *YOU* THEN!" he screamed. "The both of you can *shove* this lousy school, and its *suck* rules and regulations, so far up your constipated asses that you'll be coughin' up books for a fuckin' year!"

Eric stalked out of the door and slammed it as hard as he could. He staggered to the frat house in a total state of shock.

"Those cocksucking *assholes!*" he screeched.

How in the hell could this be happening?

Didn't those dumb shits know he was the next Montana? He shook his head in disbelief. Was *he* the only sane person left in the world? He was the best Goddamn QB this stinkin' town ever saw.

He went into his messy room and flopped down on the bed trying to get his wits about him. The shrill ringing of the telephone almost sent him through the ceiling.

He snatched up the phone. "Yeah, waddaya want?"

"Eric, this is your father."

"Dad! Uh…hi, how are ya?" he mumbled.

Great. He needed to hear from his Dad like he needed to get kicked in the balls.

Montgomery Robinson was not a happy man. "Eric, what the *hell's* going on? We received an earful from Dean Pruitt, and Mom's been locked in our bedroom crying ever since.

"What were you *thinking*? Your mother and I did not raise a drug-dealing cokehead! You're lucky Pruitt didn't call the cops on you! Jesus!" he exclaimed. "How stupid can you *be*? When are you *ever* going to grow up?"

Eric bit back a smart-ass reply. He could always count on his father to dump on him any chance that he could get. "It's not like they said, Dad. I was framed. I was…"

"Cut the bullshit, Eric. This is your *father* you're talking to, remember? I know you're capable of this and of a *whole* lot more.

"Hell, I've bailed your butt out of more messes then I care to recall, so don't *even* try to lie your way out of this one. Be a man, for God's sake! Admit it when you *screw* up."

"Thanks a hell of a lot for your *love* and support, Dad. I always *knew* that I could count on you."

Montgomery wanted to reach through the phone and smack his smart-ass son upside his dumb head. "Don't you *dare* turn this around on me! You have no one to blame for this debacle but *yourself*.

"What the *hell* didja do with all the money that your mother and I sent you? Put it up your nose?"

"Oh come *on*, Dad! You make me sound like some loser who has gambled his life away."

Jeez, what was with his old man anyway? He acted like he'd just killed ten people in a hold-up or something.

*He* was the one whose career was blown away. Eric felt like he should be entitled to some sympathy, not getting his balls busted by his anal-retentive father.

"Well, that's *exactly* what happened isn't it? Your football career is out the window. All of the thousands of dollars we paid for tuition was for *nothing*. I suppose hoping that you actually *learned* something is too much to wish for. Your grades are atrocious!"

Montgomery lifted a crystal decanter of bourbon and poured himself three fingers worth into a glass tumbler.

Eric gritted his teeth and forced the insincere words out of his mouth. "Look, Dad, I'm *sorry*, okay? Once I get back home, I'll start looking for a job.

"Hey! Maybe I can transfer to NYU. You know how much Mom likes me close to home."

Montgomery couldn't believe his ears. What? Was the boy completely *stupid*? He was living in a dream world.

"Eric," he said patiently. "We haven't done you *any* favors by spoiling you, and for that I *am* sorry.

"*You* however, are now an adult, and it's time you took responsibility for your actions."

Eric was suddenly in a complete panic. "What are you *talkin'* about, Dad?"

There was an ominous pause.

"You're on your own, son. Mother and I discussed it, and we've both decided that it would be a good idea for you to get your own place to live in."

Tears of anger and frustration welled up in Eric's eyes. "That's just *great*. With what money? I'm completely *broke*."

"What happened to the five-hundred dollars that we sent you a couple of weeks ago?"

Eric wanted to tear his hair out in fury. "I have my car insurance, gas, food, clothes. Things aren't free y'know."

Yeah, Montgomery did know. It was *his* Goddamn money that paid for it all!

He was fed up with his lazy kid. It was time to cut the strings, for his own good.

"I'm going to send the rest of your things to you when you get settled in an apartment. You need to get a *job* and support yourself,

Eric. Your mother and I have done our part. Now it's time for *you* to stand up on your own two feet."

"How the *fuck* am I supposed to get a place when I have no money? Huh? You just tell me how!"

"You talk to me like that again, I'll come down there and crack you in the mouth!" Montgomery shouted.

He drew in a deep breath and tried to calm himself. "I will wire you *one*-thousand dollars, Eric, not *one* penny more! You'd better use it to get a place *and* a job, or you're out on the street. I don't care. This is the *last* time I give you money, understand?"

"Thanks a *lot*," Eric said sarcastically.

Montgomery knocked back another triple. That's gratitude for you.

The kid was an ungrateful turd.

"Don't call unless you have your shit together," he snapped.

The connection went dead with a loud bang in Eric's ear.

"Sonofa*bitch*!" He screamed, hurling the phone, the nightstand, and his box of extra-lubricated rubbers through the frat house window.

# Chapter Eighteen

Anna applied a shiny coat of lipstick to her full lips and stood back to examine the results of an hour's worth of primping.

"Not too bad," she commented softly with a satisfied smile. Eric would be tapping on her door any minute and she wanted to knock the socks off of him.

She hadn't seen him in a week, and she missed him terribly. He sounded funny when he called earlier, and he insisted on coming over to speak with her and her mother. Anna hadn't a clue as to why he wanted to talk to her mother. It wasn't like they were best buddies or anything.

She shrugged her shoulders. She would find out soon enough anyway.

**\*\*\*\*\*\*\*\*\*\***

Outside, Eric sat in his prized Mustang and memorized the speech he would lay on Anna and the old bag.

He had slouched off of Litchfield campus in complete disgrace.

After receiving the thousand dollars his father had wired him, Eric had then bet the whole wad at Bay Meadows racetrack. Someone was looking out for him, because he strolled out three thousand dollars richer. He wished his tight-assed Dad could see him now.

He went to a reputable fence that his good pal, Benny, referred him to, and bought a flashy wedding ring and engagement band for a cool fifteen hundred. They were stolen of course, but how *else* was he going to get a one-carat rock at such bargain prices?

He rented a tiny one-bedroom house in an older part of town, and spent the rest of the day moving in. The following day, Eric purchased a round-trip ticket to New York.

He had a plan.

**\*\*\*\*\*\*\*\*\***

Eric crouched behind the shrubbery and watched his father and mother climb into their Mercedes and drive sedately down the block. He knew that they were going to the opera and wouldn't be back for hours.

He hunkered down and sprinted across the front lawn, leaping over the fence into the backyard.

He made his way to his bedroom window and pulled out his trusty pocketknife. Eric jiggled the knife and popped the lock off. "Just like the old days," he muttered smugly.

He was delighted that they never changed the ancient lock. A toddler could break in, for Christ's sake!

He stealthily climbed in through his window and landed on the carpet like a cat burglar. He made his way to his parent's room and went directly to the wall safe behind an oil painting.

He expertly twirled the tumbler to the right combination. He frowned. Something was wrong. Eric slowly repeated the combination again.

No dice.

"I don't fuckin' *believe* it!" he said with a harsh crack of laughter. Apparently his old man knew him pretty well. Eric thought he'd have at least a week until his father changed the combination.

A hot surge of anger coursed through him. He had counted on the money that was in the safe. Montgomery kept five thousand in there at all times, and his mother had some nice pieces of jewelry.

He sniffed around the room like a bloodhound searching for anything that was of any value at all.

No such luck.

It was just the same old dull crap that he'd seen all of his life. Suddenly, inspiration hit him like a bolt out of the blue.

He scrambled over to his mother's closet and started going through the pockets of her evening coats. Elizabeth had a habit of removing her jewelry on the way home from an evening out. She'd slip her earrings and necklace in the pocket of her coat and sometimes would forget to put them back in the safe right away.

Montgomery often chided her on her carelessness, warning her that she'd be heartbroken if she lost one of her precious jewels. Elizabeth would just laugh, and say she hadn't lost any jewelry yet and didn't plan to.

Eric was feeling his way through a black satin coat when he felt something hard and spiky at the bottom of the pocket.

"Oh my God!" he whispered in disbelieving glee. He snatched the items up and out for inspection.

"Holy shit! I hit the mother load!"

Lying in the palm of his gloved hand was a beautiful, heart-shaped diamond necklace and matching earrings. The earrings were at least a half-carat each. The necklace was truly a thing of beauty. It was his trump card if he needed one.

Eric hurriedly stuffed them in the pockets of his black jeans. He had seen enough cop movies to know that you'd have to be a dumbass if you didn't wear black. He kind of got off on his outfit, thinking that it made him look a little like James Bond.

Eric sneaked a glance in the mirror and admired himself for a while. With a satisfied grin, he strolled out of his parent's bedroom and left the same way he had entered.

# Chapter Nineteen

Eric cleared his throat nervously and rapped on Anna's door. He had snorted two lines before he left and was feeling jumpy.

Dorothy Price opened the door and pretended to be pleased to see him. "Good evening, Eric."

"Good evening, Mrs. Price. May I say you look really beautiful tonight."

"Thank you, Eric," Dorothy said dryly. He was there less than a minute and already she was sick of his smarmy compliments. "Have a seat and I'll go see what's keeping Anna."

"No need for that, Mom, I'm right here." Anna entered the room looking like a vision.

Eric silently congratulated himself on picking such a beauty. He deserved only the best, after all. He stood up.

"Hi honey. God, you look *gorgeous*!"

Anna blushed prettily. "Thanks. You look pretty great yourself."

Eric flexed his muscles a little. He never tired of getting compliments. "You're probably wondering why I wanted to speak to the both of you." *This is it Eric, don't blow it.*

He turned to Dorothy. "Mrs. Price, I'm sure you've noticed how much I love and adore your daughter."

Dorothy wanted to throw up. She had a sinking feeling she knew what was coming next.

Eric continued, with his best sincere face perfectly in place. "I know we're kinda young, but I think that a love like Anna and I have is rare. It only comes once in a lifetime."

Eric wanted to slap himself on the back. Where *did* his genius come from? It sure as hell didn't come from his father.

81

"I want to marry Anna right away. That is, if she'll have me."

"Oh, Eric!" Anna squealed, rushing towards him, almost knocking him down in the process.

He laughed and swung her up in his arms, kissing her full on the mouth. He was glad the old witch was getting an eyeful. He knew that Dorothy Price hated his guts, and the feeling was mutual.

There was nothing she could do, however. Anna was ecstatic, so she'd *have* to give them her blessing. Maybe he could squeeze a nice little wedding check out of her if he played his cards right. Eric released his glowing fiancée and decided it was time to turn on the charm.

He got down on one knee and pulled out a velvet box. He opened it and Anna let out a soft sigh. They were the most beautiful rings that she had ever seen. Dorothy thought that they were a little flashy, but the look on her daughter's face moved her almost to tears.

Eric pulled the engagement ring out and gently took Anna's hand. "Mrs. Price, may I have your daughter's hand in marriage?"

*Brilliant move, you sneaky son of a bitch.* There was no way that she couldn't give them her blessing. She'd lose her daughter otherwise.

"Yes of course, but…where will you live? *How* will you live? Not in the fraternity house?" She hoped that voicing her concerns would raise questions in Anna's mind also.

Eric was prepared for any questions that Dorothy fired at him. First things first, though. He gazed up at Anna solemnly. "Baby, will you make me the happiest man alive and marry me?"

Anna was so overcome with emotion that she could hardly talk through her tears. "Oh Eric, I love you so much. Yes, I'll marry you! Yes, I'll be your wife and love you forever."

Eric grinned and slid the ring onto her finger.

It was a perfect fit.

He rose and faced his adversary. "I want to put your mind at ease, Dorothy. I *can* call you Dorothy, right? We're practically family now. I moved out of the frat house and got us a great place. Wait until you see it. I have three thousand dollars in my account. Wait a minute…"

He pulled out a bank balance that indeed stated his account had three grand in it. What he didn't say was that he'd blown half of it on coke. "I plan on taking great care of your daughter…really, I have it all figured out."

Anna spoke up. "Yes, Mama. Don't worry. I have a great job with Henderson's Insurance. I don't intend on sitting at home doing nothing. Eric and I are a team now, and I want to help equally in the finances. Besides, money is the last thing that we have to worry about. Eric is almost signed with the Forty-Niners, aren't you, sweetheart?"

Eric felt a sharp pain kick in his belly. "Yeah, any day now," he said vaguely. He quickly changed the subject. "I thought that we'd go up to Tahoe and elope. Think about it, honey, it'll be so romantic. Just you and me in the most beautiful place in the world. We can leave in a coupla days. Whaddaya say, baby?"

Anna looked at Eric with shining eyes. "Yes, I'll do it!"

Eric glanced triumphantly at a resigned Dorothy. *I won.*

"I guess I can start calling you Mom," he stated with a cocky grin.

## Chapter Twenty

The first couple of months of married life started out great for the newlyweds. After a short but memorable wedding, they settled in to the quaint little house. Anna went to school part-time and then headed off to work at Henderson's Insurance. She loved her job. The people were friendly and her boss, Frank Henderson, was a sweetie.

Eric would come home from school in the late afternoon and they would sit down to a wonderful dinner that she'd prepared. Afterwards, they would make slow, sensual love to each other.

The house may not have had a lot in the way of furniture and appliances, but Anna made it cozy with the small savings that she had come in to the marriage with.

She couldn't get too extravagant, because money was tight. And Anna was troubled. Eric had told her that he had gotten a part-time job at school, but she hadn't seen one paycheck as of yet. Her salary barely covered the bills. They needed the money from Eric's job and fast.

She couldn't quell an uneasy finger of foreboding. She thought that by now, the Forty-Niners would have drafted Eric. He hadn't even so much as brought it up in conversation. Anna had a feeling that he was keeping something from her.

He started to change right before her eyes. He had erratic mood swings and was hyped up half the time, staying up until the wee hours of the morning. She turned at the sound of the front door being opened. Eric swaggered in with an armload full of shopping bags.

"Hey, baby! Look what Daddy got you."

Her eyes popped out. "What's all this? Did Christmas come early?"

Eric placed the bags on the small coffee table that Dorothy had given them. He laughed gleefully. He'd made a killing at the track and was feeling generous, plus he scored some primo coke and was pleasantly buzzed.

Anna picked up the packages and slowly began opening them up. There were matching his-and-her black leather jackets, a pair of snakeskin cowboy boots for Eric, a filmy black teddy for Anna, and expensive cologne and perfume for the both of them.

She blew her breath out in one puff. "This stuff must have cost a fortune! Where did you get the money to *pay* for it all?"

Anna suddenly let out a delighted laugh. "Oh, honey! Did you get the job with the Forty-Niners? You *did*, didn't you? That's why we're celebrating! Oh *Eric*, I'm so proud of you, sweetheart!" She wrapped her arms around her husband and kissed him softly on his unsmiling mouth.

Eric jerked her out of his arms in one forceful push. "No, that isn't *why* we're celebrating," he mimicked cruelly.

Anna took a step back. The hurt look on her face made Eric feel like a lowlife. "I'm sorry. I didn't mean to snap. There's just something that I've been meaning to tell you."

Eric's mind whirred on red alert. The wheels were churning, and turning desperately, as he tried to think of something…*anything* to get him off the hook. Telling her the truth was, of course, unthinkable.

"Baby, I've been set-up!" he stated dramatically. "I should have suspected something but you *know* how trusting I can be."

Anna was immediately concerned. "What's happened, Eric? You can tell me anything, you know you can." She softly stroked his arm; her jeweled eyes shimmering like aqua pools.

"I got kicked outta school. Some friends of mine were caught dealing drugs, a real no-no at Litchfield, and they also implicated *me*. Can you *believe* it? Fuckin' Dean Pruitt and Coach kicked me out today, just like that. With no warnin' at all!" Eric spluttered self-righteously.

He was warming to his story. "Now I don't get my shot playin' ball because of some jealous assholes with a score to settle."

A part of him actually believed the shit he was shoveling. It wasn't so far from the truth anyway. He *was* the victim, couldn't anybody see that?

Anna paced the floor furiously. "That's not *fair*! Why are they doing this to you? They have no *proof*, just the word of a couple of idiots who'll say anything to save their own skin!"

She was like a protective lioness with her mate. Eric didn't deserve the treatment he was getting! It was up to her to put a stop to it. She stopped pacing and faced Eric.

"We're going to that school right *now* and demand to talk to the dean. There's got to be some kind of mistake. You'd never do *anything* like that. I'll make him see that. If we don't have any luck with him, then we'll demand to see the superintendent!" she cried with a crusading light in her eye.

"Wait a minute, Anna. It's a bit more complicated than that." He wanted to stop her before she stormed into Pruitt's office like Joan of Arc. The last thing he needed was for those two to get together and compare notes. "Well…the thing is, they kinda *do* have proof, but it's not what it looks like," he added quickly.

Anna was baffled. "I don't understand, Eric. How can they have proof? You said you never did drugs."

"I don't. One of my so-called friends asked me to deliver an envelope to some guy a while back. I had absolutely *no idea* what was inside the envelope," he lied.

"Turns out this guy is some big-shot drug dealer and the money was for some coke that my asshole friend wanted. Dean Pruitt musta had somebody follow me because they took pictures of the exchange."

"Well, didn't you explain all that to the dean?"

"Yes, Anna, obviously I *did*," he sighed, as if talking to a stupid child. "He didn't believe me. He's *always* hated me, and this was his perfect opportunity to expel me."

Anna slowly sank into a chair and tried to absorb the enormity of the situation. "I don't suppose that they let you keep your job," she asked.

"What do *you* think?" he replied sarcastically.

"Eric, where's all the money you made? We really need it, honey."

He looked at her blankly for several seconds, but he couldn't think of a lie fast enough.

Then suddenly, bang!

Inspiration hit him like a brick.

"This is the kicker, baby…they withheld my earnings! Pruitt said something about a fine. I dunno, he probably pocketed it, I wouldn't put it past that asshole."

Anna glanced down at the packages. "Then where did you get the money for all of this?"

Eric exploded, "What the *hell* is this, a fuckin' inquisition or something? I got a hold of some money from a friend, and I decided to spoil us a little. Who knows when we can splurge like this again? Why do you have to turn this in to some kinda third degree? What the hell's your *problem*?"

He was getting more pissed off every second.

Jeez, he was married less than a coupla months and already she was naggin' him like a fishwife. She should be kissing his ass for buying her anything at all. Instead, he was getting his balls busted and he didn't like it one bit.

Women. He'd never figure 'em out.

Anna jumped out of the chair and pointed her finger at him. "Don't you *yell* at me! It was a logical enough question, wasn't it? You come in here with a bunch of expensive stuff that costs God knows *how* much.

"Can you really blame me for wanting to know how you got the money to *pay* for it all?"

Eric stalked to the refrigerator, cracked open a beer and took a long swallow. "I don't need your permission *or* your approval for anything I do, okay? If I decide to buy something, I'm gonna do it, and I don't wanna hear you yap about it either."

Anna was incensed. Here *she* was, working and going to school, paying the bills, doing *all* of the housework, and he had the nerve to act like a caveman and expect *her* to sit back and put up with it? Well, he was in for a shock.

"Don't you *dare* you say that to me! Are you the one who pays the bills? We need money, Eric. Don't you *understand* that? How could you have been so irresponsible to blow all that money on fancy things that we don't even need? It should have been used to pay for our living expenses…"

The brutal slap across Anna's face took her completely by surprise and knocked her to the ground. She cradled her hand against her cheek and stared uncomprehendingly up at him. Her face was throbbing painfully and already she could feel it start to swell.

Eric stood over her breathing harshly. "Don't you ever, *EVER* disrespect me like that again, you hear? I'm the man, and *I* make the rules, not *you*. I don't need you making me feel like shit because you pay a few lousy bills."

Anna tamped back her tears. Eric had *never* hit her before. Was this the way it was going to be from now on?

She had to get out of the house and think. She got up stiffly and walked around Eric to the front door.

"Oh no, you don't," Eric grabbed her wrist and yanked her back. "You're mine and you're not goin' *anywhere!*"

"Leave me *alone*, you bastard!" she shouted.

Anna managed to knock Eric off balance and scramble out the door. She ran about three blocks before she became winded and stopped.

Her cheek felt like it was going to explode from the pain. Anna felt light-headed and shaky.

She slumped onto the sidewalk sobbing. A car pulled up to the curb and an elderly couple peered out at the young girl crying her heart out.

"Are you okay, miss?"

Anna sprang to her feet in embarrassment. She must have looked like a crazy person or something. "Uh…I'm okay, I'm just…"

"Do you need a ride somewhere, dear?" The old woman interrupted gently. The ugly bruise on the beautiful girl's face told her all that she needed to know.

"Perhaps the hospital, or maybe your parents'?" Inquired the dapper old gentlemen.

He was in full telepathic accordance with his wife of fifty-one years. This little lady needed her folks, if she had any.

Anna wiped the tears from her face and approached the car. "Yes, I'd appreciate a ride to my mom's. She lives over on Williamsburg Avenue, if it's no bother."

"No, miss, it is no bother at all. Hop in."

# *Chapter Twenty-One*

Anna thanked the couple again, and quietly let herself into the condo. She prayed that her mother would be asleep, so she wouldn't have to face her until the morning.

"Anna? Honey, is that you?"

No such luck.

"Yes, Mom, it's me. I'll be upstairs in my room. We'll talk in the morning." She tried to bolt up the stairs before her mother ambushed her, but it was in vain. Dorothy came hurrying in from the living room.

"Hey, wait a minute. What's the rush?" She stopped short and put a hand to her throat.

"Oh my *God*! What happened to your face?" She softly probed the large purple bruise while Anna stared down at the cream shag carpet and tried to will her tears away.

"I'm okay, Mom, really."

Dorothy brushed aside the wobbly statement. "You don't look *okay* at all. Tell me how you got that bruise."

A fierce anger pulsed inside her head. That horrible bruise on her child's face was hand-sized...the *exact* size of her scumbag son-in-law's hand.

Anna looked up at her mother and dissolved. "We had a terrible fight. It was awful, Mom...it was really awful." She wrapped her arms around Dorothy and sobbed her heart out.

Dorothy cradled her only child in her arms and rocked her like she did when she was a little girl. "It's all right, sweetie. Everything's going to be just *fine*. I'm here, and I always will be. I don't want you to waste any more tears on him. I want you to get undressed and get into bed. I'm going to get you some ice for your face."

Anna stepped back and managed a tremulous smile. "That sounds good. I'm wiped out."

**********

She had just settled under the covers when she heard arguing downstairs. Her whole body tensed with the effort to hear what was going on. Suddenly she heard the stairs being taken two at a time with her mother's angry voice following closely behind.

Eric burst into her bedroom with a tragic, tear-stained expression on his face. He raced to her bedside and laid his head on her lap, sobbing loudly. "Anna, sweetheart, please forgive me, *please*...I never meant to hurt you, I *swear* it! I love you so much, you gotta believe me. I worship you!"

Dorothy wished that she had kept a pistol in the house, because she surely would have shot his lying, phony balls off. "I think you should leave now. Anna is in no shape to deal with *you*," she said coldly.

Eric's response was to cry even louder and wrap his arms tightly around Anna's waist.

Anna sat paralyzed, unable to do or say anything. She looked down at Eric's blonde head on her lap, and her first impulse was to stroke his sun-streaked hair. Instead, she clenched her hands tightly at her sides.

He looked into her turbulent blue eyes for any sign of softening. "I could cut my hand off for hitting you, baby. I was just so hurt..."

"Oh come *on*," Dorothy sneered. "You're not the one with a huge bruise on your face, now *are* you?

"Give me one good reason why I shouldn't call the cops right *now,* and have them throw your ass in jail!"

Eric gritted his teeth. If he *were* going to jail at all it, would be for the murder of his hated hag-in-law. "Because I love your daughter with all my heart."

"Spare me," Dorothy replied bitterly.

Eric turned back to Anna. The old bitch wasn't going to help him at all. "Please, honey," he whispered softly. "Give me another chance."

He gently looped her hair behind her ears and gazed solemnly into her eyes. "I love you so much. I can't live without you. I would *die* without you."

Anna was weakening slightly. "You hurt me, Eric," she whispered. "I never would have believed that you had that kind of violence in you. I'm *scared*."

Eric saw his opening and wasn't about to blow it. "I know I blew it big-time, it's just I had such a traumatic day, what with getting kicked out and all. I know it's no excuse, Anna, but I'll spend the rest of my life making it up to you. You'll never have to be scared again. I promise."

Anna caught her lower lip between her teeth, she wanted with all of her soul to believe Eric, but she had serious doubts. "I don't know," she breathed.

"Before you say anything," he interrupted, "I wanted to give you this."

He pulled something out of his pocket and had it clenched in his hand. Dorothy tensed. Whatever it was, she had the disheartening feeling that Eric was going to slither off the hook, yet again.

"I was going to wait to give you this on our first anniversary, but I want you to know just how much you mean to me.

"This was my grandmother's. She left it to me when she passed away. She wanted me to give it to the woman that I love. And that's you, Anna."

He opened his hand and let the necklace drop and dangle from his forefinger. The exquisite, heart-shaped, diamond necklace blazed with fire and light.

"Now that you have my whole heart, you can wear it close to your own."

Eric waited breathlessly for her reaction. He was glad he didn't succumb to temptation and sell the damn thing. It was his ace in the hole.

The bit about it being his grandmother's was a stroke of genius on his part. He knew by the constipated look on Dorothy's face that he had scored major points.

"I *want* to believe you," Anna said softly.

Eric undid the clasp of the beautiful necklace and put it around her neck. "Believe me, sweetheart, because I love you *totally* and completely." He kissed her lightly on the lips, just before doing the tiny clasp.

Before Anna could reply, Dorothy spoke up. "Anna, honey, I think you should take some time out to consider things, and then make a decision without any outside pressure. You're perfectly welcome to stay here with me. This is your home."

Eric clenched his teeth. "I wouldn't pressure Anna, and her home is with *me* now," he stated tightly.

The bitch was treading on dangerous ground. Nothing or nobody was going to stand in the way of what he wanted.

Anna looked helplessly from her husband to her mother. "Maybe I *should* take a little time to think things over. Please hear me out," she said when Eric began to interrupt.

"Everything's happened so fast...I need time to sort things out. Just a few days, Eric...please. That's all I'm asking for."

Eric wanted to scream in frustration. A few days with Dorothy poisoning her mind against him, and who knows *what* would happen?

"Honey, are you sure that's what you wanna do? Don't you think it would be better if you left with me now, so we could straighten this whole thing out together?"

"Didn't you hear what she just *said*?" Dorothy coldly interrupted. "If this is an example of your not pressuring her, it leaves a lot to be desired."

Eric clenched his fists. "All right, Anna, I'll give you some time," he said softly. He leaned over and kissed her gently on the lips. "Can I call you tomorrow?"

Anna looped a strand of hair behind her ear. "Yes, of course you can...we'll talk tomorrow."

"Well, goodnight then."

"Goodnight, Eric."

Eric silently followed Dorothy downstairs to the front door.

He suddenly turned around and confronted his enemy. "Don't think for one minute that this is over. Anna is my wife and she belongs to *me*."

"Anna is her own person and she belongs to no one but *herself* and I'm going to do everything in my power to wake her up from this fantasy she has about you. You can *count* on it, Eric. I never liked you from the beginning, and I *despise* you now. You make me *sick*.

"You're nothing but a lazy, shallow, low-life *bum* who's latched on to my beautiful girl like a parasite, *using* her as a meal ticket.

"But that's going to change, starting right *now*. I'll see to it. And one other thing, if you *ever* strike Anna again, I'll press abuse charges against you so fast it'll knock you on your ass. Now you get the *hell* out of my house."

Eric glared at Dorothy with undisguised venom. "You're gonna regret every word you just said to me, you old *bitch*."

His face had suddenly changed; it was ugly with malice and hate. He leaned his face forward to within an inch of her own.

"You think you know me, you don't know me at *all*," he whispered. "*I* will win...not *you*." His voice shook with the intensity of his feelings.

He stepped back and his mask was back in place. He smiled his same charming smile; only his eyes were flat and hard. "I'll be seein' ya around, Dorothy."

The mask dropped for a split second, and the loathing she saw there made her uneasy.

He turned and walked out the door, slamming it behind him.

Dorothy quickly bolted the door and leaned against it, breathing rapidly. She was suddenly very afraid of her son-in-law.

She stood there for a while, trying to collect herself. She was shook up but not about to back down.

Years of being the sole parent and breadwinner had toughened her considerably. She wasn't going to go to pieces because Eric had more or less threatened her. If he so much as tried to hurt her or Anna, she'd get the police involved immediately.

She made her way upstairs, feeling a lot better.

"Just let the little shit *try* to make a move on me, and he'll rue the day he was born," she muttered.

# Chapter Twenty-Two

Dorothy let herself out of the condo quietly the next morning. She checked on her daughter before she went downstairs, and she was sleeping peacefully, thank God.

It wasn't light out yet, and she shivered against the cold and dampness. She made her way down the deserted street in her late model Honda, thinking about Anna and how she could extract her from this disaster of a marriage. The problem was how to do it.

She couldn't force her. She *was* of age. Anna could be very stubborn when she wanted to be, and putting down Eric would lead her right back into his arms once again.

Dorothy tightened her lips. She would not allow that to happen. Now that Anna was home, she wanted it to be a permanent arrangement.

She looked into her rearview mirror and squinted at the bright headlights behind her.

The jerk had had his highbeams on for a while now.

Dorothy sped up to get away from him. The car behind her sped up as well. "Oh yeah, buddy, two can play at that," she whispered.

Dorothy floored it and shot away from the car.

Quick as a flash, the car was right behind her once more, their bumpers almost touching. There was something menacing about the car, but she couldn't put her finger on it.

She sped up yet again, but the car was right on her tail, bumping her slightly from behind, causing her car to swerve dangerously near the edge of the steep cliff.

A fine layer of sweat broke out all over her body. This person was nuts. All Dorothy wanted to do was to get away from him.

She maneuvered her way through the winding road at breakneck speed, but still the car was glued to her bumper, its highbeams blinding her. Dorothy was white with fear. She suddenly realized who was behind the wheel of the car.

She also knew with sudden clarity that he wanted her dead.

*You're gonna regret every word you just said to me, you old bitch.*

"Oh my God," she moaned.

Dorothy gripped the steering wheel and fought for command of her car. The curves were getting sharper, and she didn't know how much longer she could keep it under control.

The Honda skidded dangerously close to the guardrails, scraping up against them and causing a shower of blue-orange sparks to cover the car. Dorothy was sobbing uncontrollably.

A hairpin turn was approaching, and she knew that she was going too fast to be able to make it safely.

She valiantly struggled with the wheel for control; the turn was coming upon them. The car behind her gunned its powerful engine and pushed her bumper.

Dorothy screamed and threw her hands up around her face.

Her last thoughts were of her beloved daughter, and how she failed to protect her from the boogeyman.

The Honda flew through the guardrail and over the side of the cliff. It free fell about one hundred feet before exploding into a fiery orange ball.

Eric sat behind the wheel of his red Mustang, grinning hugely. "It's been nice knowin' ya, Dorothy, but I think I'll take over from now on."

He laughed triumphantly, gunned the engine, and cruised all the way home with his stereo cranked.

**********

The persistent ringing of the doorbell woke Anna up with a jolt. Disoriented, she groped the nightstand for her wristwatch. It read eleven o'clock.

"Jesus," she muttered. She scrambled out of bed and struggled to put her robe on. She never slept this late.

The doorbell rang once more. "I'm coming, just hold on a minute," she called as she hurried down the stairs.

Anna opened the door and was surprised to see two policemen standing there. "Can I help you?"

"Are you a relative of Mrs. Dorothy Price?"

"Yes. I'm her daughter. What's this about?"

Anna's heart started banging against her ribs, and her breath barely escaped her lungs.

The two cops exchanged glances. The older one of the two took his hat off. "I'm sorry, miss, but your mother has been involved in a fatal car accident."

"No." Anna shook her head in denial. She had her hands in front of her face as if to ward off the unthinkable words.

"I'm terribly sorry, but her car was found at the bottom of the cliff over near Miller Road. It exploded on impact...she didn't survive, miss."

The room began to violently sway, and she gripped the door handle as if it were a lifeline.

Her mother...dead. Gone from her life forever.

*"Noooo...!"* she screamed. Anna crumpled to the floor in a dead faint, darkness descending upon her.

# Chapter Twenty-Three

*New York*
*Three Years Later*

Anna stood limply, waiting for the subway to take her home. She boarded and gratefully sank down, leaning her head against the glass. She'd had an exhausting day at work.

The phone never stopped ringing and there seemed to be one crisis after another. And her boss was a selfish, chauvinistic toad who treated her like his own personal slave.

He knew Anna needed the job, and therefore was forced to put up with his abuse. He took full and total advantage, and she loathed him for it.

Things were no better at home.

She and Eric were two different people. She didn't know him anymore. He wasn't the same man she married, or maybe he was, only she had been too blinded by love to see it. All that they ever did was fight.

That was when he was at home. Otherwise he was out gambling with friends, getting high on coke and hitting on women, in that order.

Her eyes stung with tears.

She faced his cocaine and gambling addiction long ago. As for his infidelity, it never stopped hurting her inside.

Why had she married him?

He was a vain, shallow man.

He never could hold down a job for more than a couple of months at a time. Eric was lazy and perfectly content to sit back and let her work. He spent the money as fast as she could earn it.

Any money that he ever contributed was earned by gambling, dealing, or scamming someone.

Anna had learned *never* to ask.

She should have left him a thousand times over, but she was more afraid of being alone, and of having no one. Where would she go anyway?

Her mother was all she had, and she was gone. She was ashamed that she would rather stay trapped in a loveless, abusive marriage than be alone.

Tears slipped down her face.

She missed her mother every day of her life. She couldn't believe that three years had passed already. Eric was so different back then; he was loving and supportive.

She was inconsolable after her mother had died and sank into a deep depression.

Eric had bathed her, even fed and dressed her when she seemed incapable of even the smallest task.

He took care of all of the funeral arrangements, and never left her side.

When it came time for the reading of the will, Anna was astonished to discover that her mother had left her one hundred and fifty thousand dollars.

It was a combination of life insurance and the proceeds from the sale of the condo.

A secretly elated Eric persuaded her to move to New York. "After all, baby, there's nothing to keep you here anymore," he reasoned.

So they made the big move and settled into a small house on Long Island.

Anna had a hard time adjusting to her new surroundings. Eric meanwhile, had rounded up all of his old friends, spending exorbitant amounts of money on coke and living the high life.

He had already persuaded Anna into buying him a brand new convertible, a red one, of course.

"We can't keep spending money this way, Eric," she pleaded. "We'll wind up with *nothing*!"

"Relax, baby," he crooned. "We still have plenty of money left. Can't we have a little fun?"

"This is *it*, Eric," said Anna, determined not to be swayed. "I *mean* it. That money is going into a savings account, and it's not to be touched without both of our agreement, okay?"

"Whatever you say, Anna, it's your money," Eric agreed easily.

There were ways of getting around that little agreement. He wasn't too worried. Ever since he had taken care of that old bitch, Anna had been under his complete control. And that's precisely what he counted on.

**\*\*\*\*\*\*\*\*\*\***

Eric had been secretly screwing a woman who could be a dead ringer for Anna. The resemblance was amazing.

Eve Preston was the best fuck he'd ever had. She was kinky and nasty and really knew how to get him off.

Anna was so boring and uptight in bed that he could barely get it up anymore. With Eve, he was always rock hard. Together they had conspired to get at Anna's money.

Eve had gotten her hands on some excellent forged documents, including a birth certificate, social security card, driver's license, and even a phony marriage license, claiming that *she* was Anna Robinson. She left no stone unturned.

Eve had a rap sheet a mile long and used several aliases. She was a seasoned grifter with absolutely no morals. Eve Preston wasn't even her real name.

No one knew what her real name was.

The only snag with her and Eric's devious plan were Eve's fingerprints. Eric assured her that Anna had no fingerprints of her own on file anywhere.

Eve had a folder an inch thick at the 15th Precinct downtown, which, of course, included her mug shots and print ID.

They had handled that brilliantly.

It was a simple matter, really. Eve knew a cop that was dirty, and all it took was a blowjob to get her hands on her file. She took her print ID and stole a blank card.

Now it was up to Eric.

All Eric had to do was spike Anna's iced tea with a few sleeping pills. When she was knocked out, he secretly fingerprinted her with the blank card Eve had so resourcefully provided him.

Anna was none the wiser.

Eve then returned the new card with Anna's fingerprints in to her file. All it cost her was another blowjob for the cop, and one each for two of his friends.

It was a snap.

Anna was so pathetically trusting and naive. She believed that the sun shined out of his ass.

Eric smirked to himself. Yessiree, he had latched on to a meal ticket for life.

*********

Anna let herself into the quiet house. Eric wasn't home.

Big surprise.

She was glad. She wasn't in the mood for another fight. She dropped her keys on the table and started leafing through the mail; she sighed wearily.

Bills.

They never stopped coming.

Eric was driving them further and further into debt. Anna could hardly keep up. Collection agencies had started threatening them with legal action if they didn't come up with the money that they owed.

She also started getting ominous phone calls at odd hours of the day and night. The caller claimed to be an associate of a Mr. Johnny Falcone. Eric owed this Mr. Falcone person fifty thousand dollars, and if he didn't get it...well, Anna got the picture.

She was afraid for their lives from that moment on.

Eric offered no comfort at all. He was a jumpy, nervous wreck, only thinking of himself.

She would walk into a room and find him whispering angrily over the telephone. He would hang up abruptly when he saw her, and accuse her of eavesdropping on his private conversations.

He was paranoid and strung-out. The coke no longer gave him the feeling that it had used to. He needed more and more of it to give him that exquisite rush of pure adrenaline. His habit was an expensive one, and he would do anything, including lie and steal to feed it.

Anna never forgave him for squandering all of her inheritance.

He went behind her back, and little by little spent her mother's legacy. Anna was furious when she found out. Apparently, he forged her permission and had access to the whole account.

Since then, they didn't even sleep in the same bed together. Anything she felt for Eric had long since died. Her life was now filled with fear and despair.

She made her way into the bedroom and spotted a note propped up against the nightstand. She opened it up and read it in disbelief.

The note fluttered from her numb fingers onto the floor. Anna stood, rooted to the ground.

She was all alone now.

There was no one she could turn to. Her fate was sealed.

# Chapter Twenty-Four

*New York City*
*The Present*

Dominic sat behind his desk with his feet propped up. He was going over quarterly reports, but his mind was elsewhere.

Anna was not what he'd expected. He had expected a hard, calculating bitch. Someone just like Robinson himself. So far, she didn't seem to be any of those things.

She seemed soft and vulnerable.

Dominic gritted his teeth. He wasn't going to be fooled by her. She was putting on an Academy Award-winning act. He knew she had a record. Shoplifting, extortion, theft, passing bad checks, the list went on and on. Living with Robinson had certainly rubbed off on her.

If only she wasn't so incredibly beautiful.

She had occupied his thoughts all day long. Dominic pinched the bridge of his nose with his thumb and forefinger. He was remembering the feel of her skin against his hands last night.

It was warm and velvety soft. She smelled like flowers.

He would have liked nothing better than to have kissed her on her sweet-looking mouth, to have touched her and licked her....

"God," he groaned. He was as hard as a rock. *Damn her*.

He never spared more than a passing thought on any woman. He'd never been in love. Dominic doubted it existed for him.

There was no one who could fill the emptiness that was always inside him, or take away the ache in his heart. Everyone he'd ever loved was taken away from him, so he vowed he would not love.

Ever.

He would not open himself up to that kind of pain again. It almost destroyed him the last time. He was in control of his emotions now, and he wouldn't allow anyone to get too close.

So what if Anna appeared warm and genuine?

He knew from experience that appearances could be deceiving. People cloaked their true colors in many ways.

Dominic hardened his heart, not allowing himself to feel anything for Eric's woman.

He had waited too long for this, and nothing was going to deter his plans.

Nothing.

**********

Anna spent the day getting acclimated to her new surroundings. Mrs. Porter had found Anna in the atrium, staring pensively out at the ocean.

"A penny for your thoughts."

Anna turned around and saw a pleasant-faced woman smiling at her warmly at her.

Her red hair was pulled into a loose bun at the nape of her neck. It must have been fiery once, but age had mellowed it to a soft auburn, with silver streaks running through it. Her blue eyes had attractive wrinkles at the edges, as did her mobile mouth.

Katherine Porter was a happy, contented woman, and it showed. She had a crisp white apron tied around her slim waist, and under it she wore a navy blue dress. She smelled like cinnamon and warm bread.

Anna was comforted by the older woman's presence.

"Hello," she began tentatively. "You must be Mrs. Porter. I…Mr. Lockwood had said that you might show me around a little?"

Katherine nodded and folded her hands in front of her. "It would be my pleasure, dear. And please call me Katherine. I know that this big old house must be a little overwhelming, but don't you worry, we'll take good care of you," she beamed. "Why don't you go change, and then I'll take you on the grand tour."

The kind woman warmed Anna. "Yes, I'd like that very much," she said softly.

*********

The day went by rather quickly after that. Katherine had shown her every inch of the large estate.

They never did venture outside, but she promised Anna that as soon as the weather improved, they would go exploring.

Anna had a lovely afternoon, and she and Katherine became fast friends.

Later, when she returned to her suite, she found a note on her bed from Dominic, requesting her presence at eight o'clock for dinner.

A shiver went through her.

Dominic was in her bedroom, again…and without her knowledge.

********

Anna sat in front of the vanity in a sheer silk teddy and stockings. A beautiful gown in midnight blue lay across her bed, waiting to be slipped on.

She applied her make-up with a shaky hand. She had been getting ready for over an hour. The effort was well worth it.

The woman that she saw in the mirror was indeed beautiful. She wore her hair in a loose topknot, with satiny wisps of hair framing her face attractively.

Her aquamarine eyes really needed no artifice; she had a touch of mascara and eyeliner. She was luminously pale, except for her lips, which were a vivid red.

The effect was dramatic.

Anna noticed her trembling mouth, and willed herself to calm down. She rose from the vanity and slipped in to the gown. She turned around and gasped softly in the mirror.

Was this elegant woman *really* she? Anna touched the cool glass with her fingertips.

The tiny antique clock on the nightstand delicately chimed.
Eight o'clock.
She stepped away from the mirror and drew a trembling breath.
There was no putting it off any longer. It was time to face Dominic.

# Chapter Twenty-Five

**Tijuana, Mexico**

The sluggish ceiling fan in the run-down bar barely disturbed the thick, blue cigarette smoke that permeated the place. It certainly didn't improve the air quality. The seedy dive smelled like unwashed bodies, stale sweat, and urine.

The clientele wasn't much better. A scattering of disreputable men and a few broken-down whores were seated here and there.

All had the same vacant, hopeless look about them. They had reached the end of the line, and they knew it.

The man hunched over the grimy bar was a shadow of his former self. His shirt and pants were filthy and ill-fitting. Sweat rings the sizes of Frisbees were underneath his armpits. His oily hair hung in greasy ropes around his gaunt face.

He looked liked he'd aged twenty years.

Liquor and drugs took a heavy toll on the once-handsome face of Eric Robinson. But as far as he was concerned, he was lucky to be alive.

"Hey…bartender…gimme another tequila," he slurred rudely.

The unsmiling bartender silently poured another shot. "You got money to pay, *cavrone?*"

"Don' worry about it!" shouted Eric belligerently. He threw down a few crumpled dollars. "Just gimme the fuckin' drink!"

The bartender glared at Eric and slammed the drink down.

Eric downed the shot in one gulp.

His bloodshot eyes cut around the room, hoping to see a sucker that he could scam. No such luck, they were all a bunch of fuckin' losers. He couldn't believe his life had come to this.

There was only one person who was responsible for his sorry state.

Dominic Lockwood.

Hatred burned like battery acid in his gut at the mere thought of him. Everything in his life was going pretty good until that son of a bitch came along.

Looking back on it now, he was a fool to have been taken in by him. But how was he to know Lockwood was setting him up?

# Chapter Twenty-Six

***New York City***
***The Past***

There he was, sitting in an upscale bar in the city, minding his own business, when a well-dressed yuppie sat down next to him and struck up a conversation.

He reeled Eric in like a prize sea bass, expertly bringing the conversation around to business, saying how swamped they were at his office and how desperate they were for sharp, young go-getters.

He casually asked if Eric was in the market for an exciting new career opportunity.

Eric, lazy by nature, half-heartedly said he might be. It depended on what the job entailed. He certainly wasn't gonna bust his ass at some boring office job.

He was perfectly content to sit back and let Anna do all of the work. Besides, he did all right at the track, and he had a lucrative little drug dealing business on the side.

The guy was persistent though, insisting that Eric come in for an interview. It never entered his mind that the whole thing was a scam, and that Mr. Yuppie was actually a paid private investigator.

So, like a dumbass, Eric agreed to come in the next day and talk to the guy's boss, Dominic Lockwood.

Lockwood Investments occupied the top five floors in a modern high-rise on Wall Street. Eric stepped off of the elevator into the lobby and checked out his surroundings.

Expensive tapestries scattered casually here and there, covered the blonde hardwood floors. Real brick walls, mellowed with age, were a soft rose color. Indoor trees and plants, in huge brass pots, grew in abundance everywhere. Contemporary art, in black and white, adorned the walls. The atmosphere was one of total harmony. Hip, young professionals co-existed peacefully with each other in a cheerful work environment.

Eric straightened his tie and strutted to the receptionist desk. A cute redhead looked up from her terminal with a lovely smile.

"Can I help you?"

Eric flexed his shoulders a little. "Yeah, pretty lady, you sure can. I have an appointment with Dominic Lockwood."

"Oh, you must be Eric Robinson. Mr. Lockwood is expecting you. If you go straight down that hallway, you'll take the private elevator to the top. You can't miss it."

Eric smiled charmingly, "Thanks, darlin'. You know…you're wasting your time behind that desk. A pretty little thing like you should be on magazine covers."

The cute redhead blushed prettily. "Why, thank you," she cooed. "Maybe we could discuss it over drinks."

Women.

They were easy.

Throw a worthless compliment their way and they were ready to screw your brains out.

"Maybe we will. Straight through there, you said?"

**\*\*\*\*\*\*\*\*\*\***

Eric entered Dominic's penthouse suite and was told to have a seat by an imperious silver-haired, expensively dressed older woman.

Slightly miffed, he did as he was asked. Five minutes turned into fifteen, then twenty-five. The thirty-minute mark rolled by, and Eric stood.

*This is a buncha bullshit!*

"Uh…*excuse* me? I don't have all day to fart around here! How much longer do I have to wait?" he complained.

Miss Uptight Old Bitch glared at him like he was the scum of the earth. Just then, the intercom buzzed. "Mr. Lockwood will see you now," she said haughtily.

Dominic Lockwood's office was huge. It was handsomely appointed in dark cherrywood paneling and furniture. The view of Manhattan was incredible.

The man himself sat behind a massive, handcrafted desk. The sun was directly behind him, so all that Eric could see was a dark outline.

"Come in, Mr. Robinson."

"Yeah…sure," Eric mumbled.

The voice was deep and ominous.

As he made his way across the room, Eric was struck by the size of the man.

Dominic Lockwood was leaning back in a large leather recliner. One leg was across his lap while the other was swiveling the chair slightly to and fro.

His elbow was resting on the arm of the chair, and his forefinger ran alongside his face while his thumb supported the underside of his jaw.

He sat silently, watching Eric advance towards him, his eyes tracking his every movement. His face gave nothing away.

A slim cheroot was burning in a marble ashtray. The blue smoke was curling around Dominic's head like a sinister cloud.

"Have a seat," he said, with his voice pitched dangerously low.

"Yeah, sure." Eric plunked himself down on the easy chair, with his legs sprawled arrogantly out in front of him.

"You're repeating yourself, Mr. Robinson." Dominic smiled slightly, but there was a definite edge to it.

"Huh?" Eric said, taken aback.

"Is there something wrong with your hearing as well?"

Lockwood was staring at him with an intensity that was uncomfortable, and if he didn't know better, he'd swear that he had just insulted him.

"No, there isn't," he said abruptly. "So…" he spread his hands apart. "You have a job opportunity for me?"

"Maybe. That depends on you, Mr. Robinson. It depends on how much you want it and how smart you are."

"Look," interrupted Eric, more than a touch irritated. "*Enough* with the Mr. Robinson already. He was my father. Just call me Eric, okay?"

Dominic stopped the gentle swaying of the chair. He looked penetratingly at him for a few seconds.

It took all of the self-control that he had not to reach across the desk and snap his neck like a chicken. Dominic prayed that he had the patience to go on with the charade.

"Very well. Eric it is, then." Dominic pulled his lips back in a poor imitation of a smile.

The effect was frightening. It looked like the eerie, blank smile on a skull.

Eric gaped at him in horror. The dude was a fuckin' *nut*. He wanted no part of him.

He looked just like the Devil with his long spooky hair and beard, was the size of a freakin' giant, and frankly, Eric had had enough weird shit for one day.

"Uh…ya know what? I've changed my mind. I'm really not interested at all. I'm *outta* here!"

"Just a moment, Eric," replied Dominic softly.

He had to tread *very* carefully. He was fully aware of how his appearance put some people off. And that was in the best of circumstances. He had to cloak his emotions better, before his plan was shot to hell.

"Don't leave before you hear me out."

Eric stood uneasily for a moment.

"Yeah, okay," he sat down again. "So what's this great job? And, for your information, I have a great deal of experience in investments."

Actually, he didn't know squat about investments, but he sure as hell wasn't about to admit it. He was a born liar.

Dominic sat up straight and folded his hands on top of his desk. "What I'm proposing has absolutely nothing to do with investments. It's a personal matter that requires some delicate handling. It has to be done in complete secrecy by someone smart. Someone who knows how to keep his mouth shut.

"Does that sound interesting to you so far?"

Eric looked keenly at Dominic. "Go on."

The very deviousness of it appealed to Eric immensely.

Dominic continued. "I'm being blackmailed, and the party wants a quarter of a million dollars in exchange for sensitive information that was stolen from my safe. I need a man to make the drop and collect what's mine. It's that simple."

Eric liked the sound of the illicit caper better and better.

"Uh, lemme think about it and get back to you." He stood up and started for the door.

Dominic gritted his teeth, but managed a charming smile. "Don't take too long, Eric. A high paying job like this comes around only once."

Eric stopped and turned around. "How high? Exactly how much are we talkin' about?"

"Fifty-thousand dollars."

Eric was flabbergasted. "Holy shit! Are you *kiddin'* me?"

Dominic smiled in triumph.

He finally *had* the greedy son of a bitch.

It made him sick to his stomach to be offering such a ridiculous amount, especially to a low-life maggot like Robinson. He obviously thought that Dominic was a chump.

"No, I assure you, I'm not. You got a beeper number?"

Eric nodded, "Yeah, gimme a pen." He scribbled the number down on a book of matches and slid it across the desk.

"I'll call you tomorrow at noon with the details. All you need to do is follow the instructions. Think you can handle it?"

Eric smiled a shit-eating grin. "Oh, I think for fifty Gs, I'll be able to handle it just *fine*. You got yourself a deal."

As soon as Eric left, Dominic set his plan into motion.

Breathing deeply, he leaned back in the chair. He reached into his pocket and pulled out Jenny's four-leaf clover bracelet. It twinkled in the sunlight as he held it by his forefinger.

"Jenny," he whispered, clenching the bracelet in his fist.

The past rushed at him like a freight train, along with the pain and fury. Whoever said that revenge was best served cold was dead wrong.

**\*\*\*\*\*\*\*\*\*\***

Eric strolled out of the building feeling like a king. He must have really impressed that freak Lockwood. The guy was beggin' him to take the job. Shit, he'd sell his mother for fifty grand. He began to think about all of the ways that he was gonna spend his ill-gotten lucre.

Little did he know it was the beginning of the end of life as he knew it.

# Chapter Twenty-Seven

## *The Set-up*

Sure enough, Eric's beeper went off at noon, straight up. He sat in his car and snorted the last of an eight ball. A little toot was all he needed to get all the cylinders runnin' right.

He picked up his cell phone and punched out the number. Dominic answered on the first ring.

"Yeah?"

"It's me. What's the plan?"

"I want you to drive out to Harlen's Industrial. You know the place?"

"Yeah, I do. Been shut down for years now." He did drug deals there from time to time. The place was deserted and out of the way. An excellent location.

"Good. Once you get there, drive straight through the gate and park behind the old air-conditioner housing. When you get there, call me."

"Got it." Eric hung up and headed out.

Harlen's Industrial was an old paint factory. It stood like a hulking, rusted-out dinosaur.

It was an ugly, faded gray, with broken windows and rust stains dribbling down the sides of the corrugated siding. Overgrown weeds, littered with cigarette butts and beer cans, surrounded the factory.

It was depressing and desolate.

Eric rolled in and parked behind the air-conditioner housing just as Dominic said. He punched out the number and waited.

"Okay, I'm here."

"Get out of your car and you'll find an old fifty gallon paint drum.

It'll be upside down. You'll find a silver briefcase underneath it. Take it, and go into the factory.

"Once you're inside, you'll see an office to your left. Go in and sit tight until I call you back."

"Got it."

Eric hung up and got out of his car. Sure enough, there was the old paint drum upside down. Eric squatted down and gingerly lifted it. The metallic case shone dully in the sunlight. He reached in, grabbed it and quickly walked into the factory.

The place smelled old and musty. There were cobwebs everywhere. His footsteps echoed loudly throughout the place. He located the office easily, went in and turned the switch on a floor lamp, hoping it would work. As luck would have it, it did.

*Much better*, he thought to himself. *Not so creepy*.

He sat down on a rickety swivel chair. There was also a broken down desk, and he placed the briefcase on top of it.

Now all he had to do was wait.

He eyes kept landing on the case. His knees were bouncing up and down rapidly. There was a quarter of a million dollars in there. God, what he could do with all of that money.

He lightly ran his hands over the slick, smooth surface of the metal. They toyed lightly with the lock. He was sure that the case was locked. Lockwood would have to be a dumbass not to. Still, it wouldn't hurt just to check it out.

As Eric sat in the office, little did he know that located in the innocuous floor lamp, was a tiny surveillance camera filming his every move.

**\*\*\*\*\*\*\*\*\***

"Come on, you bastard. Look inside the case. You know you're dying to," Dominic whispered.

He was on the other side of the factory, watching Eric, in a state-of-the-art surveillance van that his best friend, Inspector Nick Rossi, had let him borrow.

In return, the Widow and Orphan Fund was twenty-five thousand dollars richer.

Nick knew how to finagle. Not too hard though, Dominic had done it gladly.

"Come *on* Robinson, take the fuckin' money."

Eric licked his dry lips like a lizard. His fingers were practically twitching. Finally, he couldn't take it anymore. He reached over and popped the lock.

It opened!

Eric nervously looked over his shoulder, expecting Lockwood to come bursting through the door. He slowly opened the case and sucked in his breath sharply.

Money.

Stacks and stacks of it. More money than he'd ever seen in his life. Crisp, one hundred dollar-bills in neat one-inch thick piles held together by rubber bands. His hands shook as he caressed it, as he would a lover. It would be so easy just to pick up the case and disappear.

He could start a new life, anywhere he wanted. He might even take Eve along for the ride. Anna never even crossed his mind. He sat there, chewing on the possibility of actually doing it.

Shit, if he left right now, he'd be miles away before that idiot Lockwood even knew that he was gone.

He should do it!

After all, who in their right mind would entrust a complete stranger with all of this cash? Eric wouldn't, that was for sure.

Lockwood should have known better. It was *his* fault.

He drummed his fingers impatiently on the desk and gnawed on the inside of his lip. The more he thought about it, the more convinced he became that it would all work out in his favor.

"Fuck it, I'm *doin'* it." Eric closed the case with a sharp snap and bolted from the room.

Inside the van, Dominic felt a wave of pleasure rush through him. He knew the greedy cocksucker would take the money and run. He wouldn't run far though. Dominic placed a tracking device underneath

Eric's convertible. He would know everywhere that Eric went from this point on.

Eric jumped into his car and sped off like a bat out of hell, leaving a cloud of dust in his wake. As he sped by, Dominic waited a few minutes, then pulled out smoothly and began tracking him.

*********

"Yaaaa*hoooo!!!"* Eric screamed in glee.

He was really doin' it! He had a freakin' fortune, and he didn't know what to do first. Should he go home and pack a bag, get a few things together?

No. Better not.

He might run into Anna. He had no intention of sharing the cash with her, the uptight bitch. All she ever did was nag him. He was finished with her. She'd outlived her purpose.

Hmm…but he *did* have a one hundred thousand dollar life insurance policy out on her. Maybe she oughta have a little accident. Eric quickly banished the thought.

No time.

He needed to get the hell outta Dodge.

He *did* have time to get some nose though. A coupla eight balls should tie him over for a few days. He headed in the direction of his favorite dealer.

**********

Dominic watched as Eric strutted into a clapped out structure laughingly called a house. The place was a run-down mess.

Vicious pit bulls with leather spiked collars, roamed around the tiny front yard, barking and snarling at anyone stupid enough to pass by. A chain link fence surrounded the whole place.

He quickly climbed out of the van and sprinted across the street. Luckily, Robinson wasn't a complete moron and parked a ways down the block. He pulled out a Slim-Jim from his coat pocket and broke into Eric's car in about six seconds flat.

He reached under the seat and pulled out the briefcase, then dropped something on the front driver's seat. He casually walked back into the van and waited.

Eric walked briskly back to his ride, whistling a little tune. The coke surged through his bloodstream like fine wine. He opened the door and noticed a piece of paper on his seat. Frowning and cutting his eyes in all directions, he picked it up and read.

*YOU'RE A DEAD MOTHERFUCKER. REGARDS, DOMINIC.*

"No! Oh, holy *shit!*"

He reached frantically under the seat. The case was gone.

"Oh my God," he whispered in abject terror.

He looked up and down the street, but there was nothing out of the ordinary. He couldn't see Lockwood anywhere.

He clamped his hands to his head and tried to think of a way to save his skin. He jumped in his car and burned the tires, laying about ten feet of smoking rubber on the street.

The car fishtailed wildly and sped off.

Eric Robinson was running for his life.

# Chapter Twenty-Eight

***Tijuana, Mexico***
***The Present***

Eric remembered everything like it was yesterday. Dominic played him like a sucker.

He wound up in a parking garage, with Lockwood hot on his heels. He'd been tailing him the whole time.

And after the terrifying confrontation, in which he got his ass kicked, the bastard actually shot him.

Then Dominic surprisingly offered him the money, his freedom, and a quickie divorce, in exchange for Anna.

Eric gritted his teeth in fury. Even though he never really loved her, it still burned him that Lockwood had probably screwed her eight ways from Sunday by now.

Anna was *his* woman, to use and abuse in any way he chose.

He shook head angrily. He was a fool to think that he could have just walked away with the money and his freedom. Dominic had only just begun to screw him over. The worst was yet to come.

**\* \* \* \* \* \* \* \* \***

***The Past***

After Dominic left the garage, Paulie the Gorilla roughly hauled Eric to his feet. He screamed in pain. He felt like someone poured gasoline on his legs and lit them on fire.

"Shut the hell up, or I'll kick ya in the friggin' balls!" shouted Paulie the Gorilla, in a thick Bronx accent.

He opened the door of the SUV and tossed him in like a sack of shit, which was exactly what Eric felt like.

But, at least he had the money. He clutched the bag like a lifeline.

Paulie drove in complete silence. He occasionally burped, and the pungent smell of garlic, salami, and cigar breath wafted through the air, making Eric want to gag.

He wisely kept his mouth shut. He wasn't in the mood to get jacked-up again.

They finally stopped at a small clinic. The place looked closed, but Paulie lumbered out of the car and banged on the door.

It opened, and a shaft of light spilled out into the darkness. Paulie and the man spoke in hushed whispers. He came back to the car and yanked open the door.

"Get out," he snapped.

"I need some help, man, I'm *hurtin'*," Eric whined.

Paulie sighed in irritation, "Christ, what a puss. Come on, get out."

He placed hands as heavy as anvils on the scruff of Eric's neck and pulled him bodily out of the car. He half-dragged Eric up the drive and into the clinic.

Paulie hurled him onto a metal examination table like a side of beef.

Eric screamed in agony; he was sick and tired of being tossed around like a rag-doll.

"Christ, will ya take it *easy!*" he screeched.

Paulie the Gorilla pointed a finger the size of a hot link at him. "You shut your pie-hole. Be grateful you're gettin seen at all."

Just then Solomon Johansen walked in and rolled his eyes to the heavens. Dominic owed him *big*-time.

"So," he said cheerfully. "What seems to be the problem?"

"What seems to be the *problem*?" Eric repeated shrilly. "Uh...*hello*...? I've been fuckin' *shot* in both my fuckin' *legs*!

*"That's* what seems to be the problem!"

Solomon was unfazed.

"Relax. They're only flesh wounds; all they need is a few stitches.

Pull down your pants and lemme take a look."

Eric struggled and finally was able to pull his pants down to his ankles. He lay down weakly on the cold table, feeling faint.

Solomon poured saline solution over Eric's legs to clean the wounds. He dabbed them dry with some gauze.

"This might hurt a bit." He began stitching up his legs.

*"Shit!* It hurts like bloody hell!" Eric screamed.

Solomon stopped what he was doing and glared at Eric.

*"Look,* you. I've had it up to here with all you're Goddamn sissy whining. If you say another word, I'll tell your friend Paulie here to beat the living *daylights* out of you...understand?"

Eric nodded and kept his mouth shut. He cut his eyes quickly over to Paulie who was sitting in a chair looking like King Kong, only uglier.

He was reading a *Playboy* and avidly picking his nose. His finger was jammed up his olive-sized nostril, ferreting out stray boogers.

Finally the ordeal was over. Eric managed to limp pitifully to the car on his own.

He gratefully sank into the plush leather seat and closed his eyes. *Soon.*

This would all be over soon, and then he'd be free...with all that money. He smiled and drifted off into an uneasy sleep.

********

"Hey...*wake* up! It's time ta go." Paulie shook Eric awake.

"Huh? Wha...?" Eric said groggily.

He winced and sat up. He had a crick in his neck and it was painful to move around. He rotated it gingerly, anxious to be getting out and on to the plane.

They'd arrived at an airstrip where a small jet was fueled and ready to take off. He staggered out of the car and boarded the plane with Paulie in tow.

The flight was uneventful and long. Eric spent the time staring out the window. Paulie the Gorilla spent his time reclined in his seat, snoring loudly.

He eventually fell asleep because he was jolted awake when the plane touched down.

The Dominican Republic, an independent nation, occupies the eastern part of the Island of Hispaniola.

It's in the center of the Greater Antilles, between Cuba and Puerto Rico. They landed in the capital city of Santo Domingo, located in the center of the south coast. It boasted a population of two million people. The lights of the city glittered like diamonds.

Eric hobbled out of the plane, breathing in the soft warm air. It caressed his face, like the velvet fingers of a lover.

"Come on, *move* it," Paulie snapped.

He gave him a shove that almost caused Eric to topple down the rest of the flight of stairs.

"Jesus!" Eric muttered in disgust.

He carefully made his way across the tarmac where a car was waiting. Paulie slid behind the wheel. They drove in silence to the Hotel Santo Domingo.

They registered and were given their room key. It was a two-bedroom suite naturally, because Paulie the Gorilla was not of a trusting nature.

Eric eased himself down on the soft bed with a groan.

Paulie deposited him in his room and dourly told him to get some sleep. "This ain't no vacation. Be ready ta go at eight in the mornin'.

"And if I catch you even *thinkin'* of anything funny...I'll kill you," he threatened.

Eric had no doubt that he meant it.

The two days passed in a blur. He was hustled out of the Hotel by Paulie and into the Dominican Notary Public Office, where he signed a complaint for a mutual consent divorce.

It was submitted to the court and a hearing was set for the following morning.

In order to get a divorce you must stay in the Dominican Republic for two days. Once your court hearing was over, you're free to leave anytime after twelve noon on that day.

He was in and out of court promptly. The proceedings went as smooth as silk.

Everything had happened so quickly that before Eric knew it, they were boarding the jet and taking off for parts unknown.

It was hard to believe that he was no longer married. He could have cared less; all he wanted was his money and his freedom.

"So, what happens next?" Eric wanted to know.

Paulie smiled. "What happens is I dump your ass off in Mexico and from there you can do whatever you like. Just remember, if I catch your face in New York, I'll make ya sorry you were ever born. You *got* that?"

"Yeah, I got it. And don't worry, I have no intention of *ever* goin' back." That of course was a lie. He wasn't going to obey that asshole Lockwood. Why should he?

He'd wait a month or so, enjoy the fine Mexican tequila and women, then creep into town as quietly as possible.

As soon as he was free of Paulie, he was going to contact Eve. She must be going out of her mind wondering where he was.

They had big plans for the fifty thousand dollars he was going to get. Wait till she found out it was a quarter of a million. Shit, she'd wet her panties!

Eric reclined his seat with a huge grin. "How long until we get to Mexico?"

Paulie looked up from yet another skin magazine. "'Bout an hour."

"Good. I can't wait. I've never been there before." He yawned a huge, jaw-cracking yawn, and promptly fell asleep.

Paulie just smiled and resumed his ogling.

**\*\*\*\*\*\*\*\*\*\***

The plane landed at a private airstrip in Mexico City. Eric unbuckled and reached for the duffel bag. "Well, I guess this is goodbye."

Paulie was picking his nails with a pearl handled switchblade and could've cared less.

"Guess so," he shrugged. "Sayonara, asshole. And don't forget what I told ya."

*Can't say it's been a pleasure, you fat asshole.* "Yeah, well it's been real," Eric mumbled.

He waited impatiently while the stairs folded down. He hobbled down them quickly and breathed in the sultry, tropical air.

He couldn't wait to check into a five star hotel, swill down a frosty beer, and find a woman.

And in that order.

He limped across the hot tarmac and into the small terminal. He made his way to customs and plunked the bag down for inspection.

A dour looking Mexican opened the bag and did a double take. He snatched up the bag and spoke in rapid Spanish.

Eric was suddenly surrounded by vicious-looking federales. He was roughly thrown to the ground and cuffed.

"Hey! What the *fuck's* goin' on?" he yelled. "Since when is it a crime to travel with money, huh? What did I do wrong?

*"What,* for Christ's sake?"

"You think you can bring your filthy drugs into this country and we do nothing?" said the meanest looking federale. "Huh, *cavrone?"*

Eric looked up at him like he was crazy. *"Drugs?* What the hell are you *talkin'* about? I don't have any drugs!

"There's two hundred and fifty thousand dollars in that bag! It's my life savings, I was gonna retire here!"

*"Silencio, pendejo!"* said Benito Escobar, a seasoned federale of ten years. *"You* are a liar!"

He threw the bag down, and Eric couldn't believe his eyes. It was filled with cocaine.

Ten kilos of cocaine to be exact. As well as a couple of pounds of pot thrown in for good measure.

The money of course, was gone.

That fucker Lockwood had set him up.

Again.

"Listen," he began desperately. "I was set up. Ya gotta *believe* me. I have *no* idea how those drugs got into my bag. My *money* was supposed to be in that bag!"

The guard hauled Eric to his feet. "Look, I can prove what I'm sayin' is the truth. I just came off that blue and white jet outside. There's a big, fat, slob on it named Paulie, *he's* the one who planted those drugs on me, I *swear* it!"

Benito glanced outside and turned his attention back to Eric. "I don't see any jet outside."

*"What?"* Eric exploded. "That's impossible, it was just there a minute ago!"

Eric looked around wildly and sure enough, the jet was gone. *This can't be happening to me.*

Benito laughed ominously. "You know what I think, *amigo*? I think you're just another lying drug dealer, and a stupid one at that.

"Did you think we would look the other way when we found the drugs? Or maybe you thought we were just a bunch of corrupt wetbacks, ripe for a bribe?"

"No, I swear…"

"Shut up, *maricone*. And do *not* interrupt me again." Benito's eyes were like black flint.

"You are under arrest for possession of illegal narcotics with the intent to sell. Ramon!" he shouted.

A young guard sprang to attention.

"Take this *gringo* away."

"God, *no!*" Eric blubbered. "Please, I'm *innocent*. Please, just *listen* to me! I was set up…I was set *up*…!"

His voice echoed through the terminal as he was dragged, kicking and screaming into a waiting police car.

Eric Robinson was well and truly screwed.

# Chapter Twenty-Nine

**Central Mexico**

"Hey, *gringo.* You have a visitor."

A swarthy guard banged his billyclub across the bars of the squalid cell Eric Robinson called home. He'd only been there for five days, but it felt like five hundred.

It was worse than anything he'd ever imagined. The prison itself was a hellhole. Unsanitary and disgusting, the inmates lived like a bunch of animals.

The place was infested with rats. Cockroaches as big as his fingers swarmed every inch of the place.

His cell had a dirt floor with a grimy mattress thrown in the corner. A bucket was his toilet. Forget about luxuries like toilet paper, fresh water and electricity. They were non-existent.

He'd hardly slept at all for fear that he'd get gang raped by the brutal inmates that looked at him like he was a piece of meat. How he'd survived up until this point was a miracle.

He jumped up from the mattress and scrambled to the guard. "Who is it?"

God, maybe by some unbelievable stroke of luck, Eve had found out about his predicament and had hired a sharp lawyer to save him from a sure death.

The guard glared at him and said nothing. He merely unlocked the cell and snapped, "Follow me."

As if he had any choice.

He was lead to a visitor's room that was amazingly clean. Obviously for the comfort of the visitors, they could give a damn about the inmates.

The room was Spartan, with only a table and two chairs in it. The guard handcuffed Eric to the chair and left, locking the door behind him.

Eric waited nervously and wished he could have had a shower. He was a grimy mess and was well aware that he stank of B.O.

He hoped with all his might that a lawyer was going to walk through the door and get him the hell out of here. He didn't know how much longer he could survive on the inside.

He waited another ten anxious minutes before he heard keys unlocking the door. He sat up and waited expectantly.

When he saw who it was, he slumped in his chair and was rendered momentarily mute.

Dominic Lockwood strolled in, looking cool and immaculate in cream linen pants and a silk shirt. His coal black hair was pulled back in a sleek ponytail.

He sat down and crossed one elegant leg over the other. He held Eric's stare for a few beats then pulled out a slim cheroot and lit it, blowing the smoke directly in Eric's face.

"Hello, Robinson," he said pleasantly. "Enjoying the accommodations?"

Eric jerked spasmodically, trying to lunge across the table to get at Lockwood. The handcuffs shackled him down like a dog.

"You fucking *cocksucker!*" he yelled. His face was mottled purple with rage. Spittle flew everywhere.

"You set me up, you *asshole!* Right from the *first* time we met. You never had any intention of giving me that money!

"What the hell did I *ever* do to you, huh? Why are you *doing* this to me? *Why?*" he shouted.

"You wanna know *why?*" Dominic pulled his lips back in an awful smile. "I'll tell you *why* Eric."

His face changed, it turned into the face of a killer in the blink of an eye and it was a terrifying transformation.

His lips barely moved when he spoke and his voice was so sinister, goose bumps broke out all over Eric's body.

"Because you killed my sister."

Eric jerked his head back. "Your sister?" he said blankly.

"Wha…what are you *talking* about? You're not making any sense at all. I never even knew you *had* a sister, and I sure as hell didn't *kill* her! I've never killed anyone!"

*Except that old bitch, Dorothy.*

Dominic clenched his jaw. "You have a real lousy memory, Robinson. Either that, or you don't have a soul."

He reached in his pocket and dropped the four-leaf clover bracelet on the table.

"Recognize this?"

Something flickered in Eric's eyes. "That looks like…Uh…I…I haven't seen that in years…" he said faintly.

"Oh, come *on*. You can do better than that. Who did it belong to?" Dominic whispered darkly. His eyes glittered like quicksilver and bored a hole right through Eric.

Eric closed his eyes.

He couldn't believe his stupidity.

*They had the same last name.*

Why, oh why didn't he *ever* make the connection?

Their last name was an unusual one, he should have *known*. His past came rushing back to haunt him.

*"WHO DID IT BELONG TO?"* Dominic shouted. The tendons in his neck bulged like rope.

"J…Jenny Lockwood," Eric whispered, defeated.

"Give the man a prize!" said Dominic savagely. He had a finger hold on his composure.

"I gotta tell you, I've been searching for you for so many years, I thought I'd never find you. I've dreamt of torturing you slowly and excruciatingly a hundred times over.

"You see, Eric, even though *you* forgot Jenny and what you did to her, I never did.

"And I *never* will."

Eric swallowed nervously and licked his dry lips. "I heard about Jenny dying, I could understand why you're so upset. But, I didn't kill her. You *know* I didn't kill Jenny…I…"

"Don't you *DARE* speak her name, you son-of-a-bitch. You killed her as sure as if you held the scalpel in your hand.

"When she lay dying in my arms, the very day she told you she was carrying your child, the *same* day she went to that monster who butchered her, she told me everything that you said to her.

"Everything except your stinking name, you low-life *animal*. She died choking on her own blood, before she could tell me who you were."

He paused to draw a harsh breath. He felt as if Jenny had died all over again. He was powerless to stop the emotions from flooding through him. He was drowning in them.

Eric cleared his throat. "Look, I don't know what Jen...your sister told you, but sh...she must have been delirious.

"I was just surprised when she told me she was pregnant. We had a little misunderstanding, that's all. And she stormed off before I could apologize.

"I never told her to get an abortion. I'm not going to take the blame for that. That was all her doing..."

Dominic roared like a lion, picked up the table, and hurled it across the room. He grabbed Eric by the throat and began squeezing. "I should kill you right *now*," he snarled.

"Do you think I'd believe *anything* coming out of your stinking mouth? You desecrate my sister by lying to save your own ass!"

He tightened his hold on Eric's throat until his eyes rolled back in to his head. It would be so easy to end his miserable life right here and now, but Robinson deserved to suffer, as *he* had suffered for all these years.

He abruptly released Eric and kicked his chair over, causing him to fall painfully on his face. He lay there, shackled and gasping for air. A violent purple bruise was already forming around his throat.

"Fuck *you*, Lockwood," he coughed. "When they find out you planted those drugs on me, I'll be set free..."

Dominic's laughter rang out through the room. "Who's '*they*' Eric?" He pointed a finger towards the door.

"You mean the people here in this fine institution? Get *real*, asshole. You're never getting *out* of here. I've seen to it.

"Starting today, you're gonna be sharing a cell. I handpicked your roommate, and I know he's just dying to meet you."

He bent down and jerked the chair over so he could look Eric in the eye. "My sister was the sweetest, most gentle soul in the world. She was beautiful, compassionate and smart. She could have been anything, *would* have been, if she hadn't met *you*.

"You took her heart and soul and crushed it. You made her feel like a worthless nothing.

*"You* are responsible for her death. So now *I've* named myself your judge, jury and executioner.

"And I sentence you to life in this prison. Not that you'll live long, the inmates in here are brutal.

"But, however long you *do* live...you'll suffer.

"Just like you made Jenny suffer. Just like I've been suffering all these years. I hope you rot in *hell*."

He rose and started for the door.

"No, wait, don't go!" said Eric frantically, wiggling on the floor like a worm. "You can't leave me here, you bastard! Come back...COME BACK HERE YOU *FUCKER!*"

Dominic walked out the door and never looked back.

## Chapter Thirty

**Tijuana, Mexico**
**The Present**

Eric brooded over his whiskey. That bastard Lockwood left him there without a backward glance. His hand tightened on the glass, threatening to break it.

He was thrown back into his cell and met his new roommate, an animal that had raped him that very night.

Eric fought him off with all his strength, but to no avail. Diego Sanchez outweighed him by fifty pounds and was as strong as a bull.

From that moment on, he became Diego's personal property.

His hand shook as he raised the glass to his lips. Thank God, he only had to put up with *Diego's* sick advances, for he was very jealous and possessive, and kept the other inmates off of Eric.

He soon discovered that he had sexual power over Diego, and decided to use it to his advantage. He followed Eric around like a lovesick puppy, and before long it was Eric who had the upper hand in their relationship. Eric despised Diego, but had to pretend he enjoyed the nightly assaults. Even though he didn't know it, Diego Sanchez was going to help him escape.

**\*\*\*\*\*\*\*\*\***

The prison sat on about twenty-five acres of farmland. They grew corn, beets, potatoes and onions. The prisoners had to work in the fields picking crops.

Sadistic guards patrolled the area on horseback with rifles ready to shoot if anyone was stupid enough to try and escape.

Eric and Diego worked together side-by-side picking onions from the field. They were shirtless and sweat ran in torrents down their backs. The sun beat down mercilessly and the air was thick and humid.

It was hell on earth.

Eric had formulated a plan. He managed to steal a book of matches from one of the inmates during dinner. Not an easy task, because even looking at someone the wrong way could mean instant death.

He also found a crushed aluminum can in the exercise yard. He quickly slipped it in the waistband of his pants without anyone noticing. He made a small tear in his mattress and stuffed his little stash inside, hoping Diego or the guards wouldn't find it. Otherwise, he was sunk.

Today was the day.

Eric was going to escape or die trying.

His matches were tucked in the elastic waistband of his pants. He prayed that they were still dry because he was sweating like a pig. A strip of the aluminum beer can was resting inside his shoe, sharpened to a vicious point.

An ancient tractor squatted on the left side of the field where they were picking onions. Eric patiently waited until the guard turned his attention and quickly ran around the side of the tractor and stuffed his shirt into the fuel tank.

With trembling fingers, he lit the whole book of matches and touched it to his shirt. He prayed to God that no one would smell anything until it was too late.

When the shirt caught on fire, he ran around to where Diego was hunched over picking, and whispered, "Come on, let's get the hell outta here."

"Whachu talkin' about?" Diego looked up with a stupid look on his bovine face.

Eric looked wildly around and grabbed Diego's arm. "We're escaping, just like we've always dreamed about."

Diego leaped up, ready for action. "What we gotta do, Eric?"

Eric cut his eyes in fifty different directions. "Listen up, we have *no* time. I rigged the tractor to blow, when it does, we run like hell for the jungle. It's our only chance."

Everything happened at once.

Eric and Diego started running across the field towards the dense jungle that surrounded the prison.

A guard spotted them and raised his rifle to shoot while yelling in rapid Spanish at the same time.

The tractor exploded into a huge fiery orange ball, and the impact rocked the inmates and guards off of their feet.

All hell broke loose. Inmates were making madcap dashes for freedom, and the steady crack, crack, crack of gunfire ricocheted through the air.

All of the inmates were soon rounded up. The unlucky ones lay where they were shot, dead or left to die.

Eric and Diego were nowhere to be found.

Rafael Espinoza, the head guard, took off on horseback into the jungle, determined to capture the two prisoners.

And when he did, he'd kill them slowly for daring to escape on his watch.

*********

"Come on, Eric. This way," panted Diego.

They were at a dead run, slogging through the impenetrable jungle. Giant palm fronds slapped at their faces. They were scratched from head to toe from the thick vines that coiled around them like anacondas.

Steam rose from the ground, making it impossible to see which direction to go.

"Are you sure this is the right way?" Eric said breathlessly. His lungs felt like they were going to explode, but he dared not stop. He was sure that the guards were not far behind.

"*Si*. I *know* the way out of here…you will see, Eric. Then we will be together. Just think…" Diego stopped abruptly.

The sound of thundering horse hoofs stopped the both of them dead in their tracks.

Eric grabbed Diego by the shoulders. "Listen carefully, because we only have *one* chance. This is what you do…"

**\*\*\*\*\*\*\*\*\*\***

Rafael slowed his horse down to a trot. The jungle was alive with the sounds and smells of a thousand different creatures.

He hated it.

Sweat rolled down his forehead and into his eyes, stinging them. Even though he'd never admit it, the jungle had always scared him.

With all the steam rising from the ground, the landscape was eerie and surreal.

His horse, sensing his master's unease, whinnied and almost threw him of off his seat. "Easy, Santino, easy," he whispered.

The high-pitched scream of a monkey in the trees spooked the stallion. It reared up on its hind legs and sent Rafael flying. He landed flat on his back, momentarily stunned. His rifle lay about five feet from him.

A fatal mistake.

Diego and Eric leapt from behind a banana tree, and before Rafael could even recover, Diego snatched up the rifle.

"Remember what I told you. No noise," warned Eric.

Diego grunted and turned the rifle around butt-end. He swung up and brought it down on the face of Rafael Espinoza with the impetus of a sledgehammer.

It made a sickening crunching sound. Again and again, he slammed the rifle down until Rafael's face was a bloody, unrecognizable mush.

Breathing harshly, Diego dropped the rifle. A satisfied smile was on his face. He loved killing. He could smell the fresh blood from the dead guard and it turned him on.

Eric reached in his shoe and advanced softly behind Diego. He wrapped his arms around him and whispered, "That was excellent Diego, you saved our lives. Now we can be together."

He slipped one hand inside the waistband of Diego's trousers and began caressing him.

Diego uttered a guttural cry and grew hard in Eric's hand.

He never even felt the razor-sharp aluminum slice across his throat until it was too late.

Eric stepped away from Diego, who was clutching his throat trying in vain to stem the flow of blood. He dropped to his knees and stared at Eric uncomprehendingly.

"Did you honestly think I'd spend the rest of my life with a faggot like *you*?" Eric laughed.

"I *used* you, Diego, and like the dumbass you are, you never even saw it coming. I wouldn't worry though; you'll be dead in a minute. Then it'll *all* be over."

He walked over to the horse and mounted it smoothly. What a stroke of luck. It sure beat walking.

He glanced at Diego who lay face down and unmoving. It was time to go. Freedom was calling him.

# Chapter Thirty-One

**Tijuana, Mexico**
**The Present**

How he'd ever made it out was a miracle. After several hours of wandering through the steamy jungle, he finally reached a dirt road and almost kissed the ground.

He set the horse free, and he walked a couple of miles until he was able to hitch a ride with an old farmer who was driving into Tijuana.

He'd been there ever since, working at a greasy diner, sweeping floors and busing tables for almost nothing. He had to lay low until he figured out a way to get back into the States.

He had a score to settle with Dominic Lockwood. That fucker was gonna pay for ruining his life.

"You're gonna pay, Lockwood. Ya hear me...? Motherfuck..." he slurred.

His head dropped forward, and he jerked it upright. He had to think of a way, but his alcohol-soaked brain couldn't seem to focus.

A man a couple of chairs down shifted over until he was seated next to Eric.

He was a fright to look at.

Tall and stooped, he was thin almost to the point of starvation. His skin had the same dreadful gray pallor as a corpse. His baby-fine, red hair shot from his scalp like an electrified Afro.

But it was his face that took the prize.

The right side was a puckered mess. A long jagged scar started from the corner of his eye, and ran unevenly all the way down to his chin. His right eye drooped lower than his left, and if that wasn't bad enough it was lazy and wandered independently.

The rest of his face was acne-scarred and oily. He pretty much gave Quasimoto a run for his money.

He tipped his head toward Eric. "Did I hear you say Lockwood? That's a mighty unusual name. There wouldn't happen to be a first name to go along with it, would there?"

Eric turned and did a double take. Why the hell did he attract all the weirdos?

Was there a sign festooned around his neck that said, "Jacked-up freaks are welcome?"

"Get *lost*, asshole, I don't answer questions from strangers. Whassit to ya anyhow?"

The man tapped his face. "You see this scar here? Well, someone did this to me, and the sonofabitch's last name was Lockwood, so I just wondered if it was the same mean bastard that ripped my face."

His lazy eye twitched and floated crazily in its socket. He looked like a lunatic.

Eric leaned back and looked at him with a gimlet eye. "The dude's first name is Dominic. Dominic Lockwood."

"Big mother, right? 'Bout six foot six, or so. Built like a friggin' brick house?"

Eric nodded. "Yeah, that's *him* all right," he said bitterly.

The man slapped the bar. "Ha! I *knew* it! It sure is a small world isn't it? So what'd he do to *you*? Somethin' awful right?

"Man, oh man, how I'd love to get my hands on *that* asshole. I'd kill him with my bare hands, that's what I'd do!"

He lifted his drink to his lips and gulped. "Yessir, I'd kill him!"

Eric gnawed on his inner lip. Maybe this ugly cuss was the key to Dominic's undoing *and* his ticket out of here.

"How'd you like to help me to do just *that*? If we put our heads together, I'm sure we could figure *something* out. Trouble is, I'm a little strapped for cash."

The man, almost pathetically eager, boasted, "I got me a nice little nest egg. I might be persuaded to help you. You scratch my back and all that. I'd do *anything* to get even with Lockwood."

"In that case, consider us partners." Eric held his hand out. "We haven't been formally introduced. My name is Eric. Eric Robinson."

The man pumped his hand cheerfully. "Sheldon Leevy's the name. Nice to meetcha."

An evil smile spread across Eric's face.

An unholy alliance was about to be born. And together they would form a pact to bring Dominic Lockwood to his death.

Slowly and painfully.

He was going to return the favor and make Lockwood *pay* for every agony he'd had to endure.

Revenge was going to be so very, *very* sweet.

# Chapter Thirty-Two

**The Hamptons**
**The Present**

Anna walked slowly into the library and paused.

Dominic stood with his back to her, staring into the fire blazing behind the grate. Her eyes traveled over his body as if they had no will of their own. His broad back was powerfully muscled, tapering into his slim waist. His hands were in his pockets, drawing attention to his backside, which Anna had to admit, was pretty darn spectacular.

Dominic turned, sensing he was no longer alone. He stared at her for a long beat. "How long have you been standing there?"

There was a faint accusatory note in his tone.

Anna immediately bristled. "Not long, I *assure* you. I know, maybe I should wear a little bell around my neck, would *that* make you happy?" she snapped.

Every time she was in the same room with him, she lost her cool. She couldn't seem to help herself.

Dominic lifted an eyebrow, "You're unbelievable, you know that?"

He shook his head in disgust. "I asked you a simple question, and do I get a nice, polite answer? No...I *don't*. Instead, I get a bitchy, *smart-ass* reply!"

Anna's eyes shot angry sparks. "Well, *excuse* me! How did you ex*pect* me to react? You obviously thought I was sneaking up on you. What did you think I was going to do anyway? Stab you in the back with the fireplace poker?"

"Lady, you'll *never* get that chance." His lips barely moved when he spoke and it raised goosebumps on Anna's arms. In an instant, he was across the room and in her face.

Anna rapidly backed up until she bumped into the back of a sofa. The fear on her face was almost palatable.

"If you think you're afraid of me now, you try something cute and I *promise* you, you'll live to regret it." His eyes were flat, hard chips.

Anna swallowed down her fear. "What could I *possibly* do to a big, strong caveman like *you*? You see I'm not like you, Mr. Lockwood. I don't have to terrorize and intimidate people to make a point."

She shook her head angrily. "You know...for someone who was born with a silver spoon in his mouth, you're certainly ill-mannered and *crude*. You're nothing but a barbarian and a bully!"

Dominic smiled coldly. "You don't know a damn thing about me, so please...*shut* your mouth. But you're right about one thing. I *can* be barbaric when I'm pushed. For your sake, don't push me."

Anna shoved him away and scrambled around him. "I wouldn't *dream* of it." She tamped down her tears. "I'm going to my suite. I seem to have lost my appetite."

"Don't be silly. You have to *eat*," said Dominic, slightly contrite.

"I couldn't choke down a bite. Enjoy yourself though; you seem to have a taste for blood. The fresher the better." Anna spun on her heel and stalked out of the library.

She was sitting on the floor in front of the fireplace with her arms wrapped around her legs when Dominic quietly let himself in.

She looked small and lost.

He silently cursed himself for acting like a brute. He knew she didn't have a killer instinct, but yet he felt the need to lash out and hurt her. He wanted her to be cold and cruel. She was supposed to be a selfish user. He wanted to hate her.

He didn't.

"Anna?" he said softly.

She looked up and said nothing. She'd been crying. Her eyes were red and teary. Dominic felt ten times worse.

"I know you said you weren't hungry, but I'm not a complete savage. You're still a guest in my home, and you deserve to be treated decently. Whatever our differences may be.

"I have a tray outside your door, and I really would like it if you'd share a meal with me. *Please*, Anna."

She didn't know if it was the "please" or the formal, almost courtly way he asked that changed her mind. But she found herself nodding and accepting his offer.

"Okay," she whispered. A tentative smile was on her lips.

He smiled down at her and it was a genuine smile, full of warmth. The difference was astonishing. He was devastatingly handsome.

"Good. Stay where you are. We'll eat in front of the fire if that's all right with you."

"Yes, that would be lovely." Anna watched him walk outside her door and lift a heavy silver tray like it weighed nothing. She was struck again by his strength and virility.

The dark formal clothes he wore complemented his looks. His long black hair moved like liquid silk over his shoulders.

She felt herself falling, and was powerless to stop the feeling. This man was her enemy wasn't he? What in *God's* name was happening to her? She should hate him. He was remote and untouchable. She wanted to hate him.

She couldn't.

The food was delicious and they dined quietly, but the silence was a comfortable one.

"Everything was wonderful. I couldn't eat another bite." Anna patted her mouth with the linen napkin and placed it on the tray.

Dominic had also finished and was stretched out alongside the fireplace, sipping champagne from a long fluted glass. "I'm glad you enjoyed it. I didn't realize how hungry I was until I started eating," he quipped.

Anna smiled. "I'm sure it takes a lot of food to fuel that great big body of yours."

She immediately wished she could have taken back the words. They were much too familiar sounding. Her cheeks were burning with embarrassment. She put her glass to her lips and gulped some of the golden liquid, almost choking in the process.

Dominic laughed a little. He felt an unfamiliar thrill race up his spine. So...she noticed him on a physical level.

He wasn't conceited, but he knew his looks got attention from the opposite sex. "Yeah, I guess it does," he said softly.

His long fingers toyed with the stem of the delicate glass. He was twirling it slightly to and fro. The slightest pressure could snap it in half.

Anna stared, hypnotized. It was amazing to see how such large masculine hands could be as gentle as his were being.

"Anna...?" Dominic nudged her gently.

Anna jerked her eyes away and looked up. "What? Did you say something?"

"Only that you seemed to be a thousand miles away."

"I'm sorry. I guess I was."

"What were you thinking about?"

"Nothing...Everything." *You.*

She set her glass down carefully on the hearth and stretched out opposite him. "Last night I saw you on the beach, and I wondered what you were doing out there on such a terrible night."

Dominic stared at her enigmatically. "I saw you at your window. I hope I didn't startle you."

"No, you didn't," she said quickly. Then she smiled ruefully. "Well, maybe just a little bit. The power had just gone out and I was a bit frightened by the storm. Then I saw you...and then...and then you were gone. I almost thought you were an apparition," she laughed a touch nervously.

"When the storm knocked the power out, I took Thunder, that's my stallion, and rode out to start our back-up generator.

"I didn't want to drag William out of bed when I could do the job just as well. It wasn't anything as mysterious as your apparition though," he joked.

"Oh. Well, I *knew* there had to be a logical explanation. I wasn't afraid, just curious," she said airily.

"Oh yes, of course," he said seriously. But, there was a twinkle in his eyes. She charmed him and he decided to tease her. "Actually did Mrs. Porter tell you about Agatha?"

"Agatha?" Anna shook her head. "No. Who is she?"

Dominic drew his brows together. "Hmm…uh…just forget I mentioned anything."

"No! I don't want to forget it! Tell me, Dominic! Who's Agatha?" She had a sinking feeling that it wasn't a happy story.

Dominic sighed deeply. "Before I bought this place, it was owned by an eccentric old women named Agatha St. Germain.

"Well, I guess in her day the old gal was really quite something because she had a string of lovers. One for every day of the week."

Dominic looked up at Anna, who gazed at him spellbound.

He fought back laughter and was sure he'd bust up before he finished spinning the outlandish tale.

"Well?" She demanded. "Don't stop *now*! Go on, finish the story!"

Dominic continued. "As I said before, the old bat was hot, and finally she met her true love. His name was Senior Don Juan de la Cruz. He was this famous bullfighter in Spain.

"Well, old Don Juan was quite the lady's man and he cheated on her any chance he could get. Agatha was insanely jealous and told the Don that if he cheated on her just *one* more time, it was curtains.

"He should have took her at her word because the unthinkable happened." He paused dramatically. "And it happened in this *very* room," he said ominously.

Anna put a hand to her throat. "Wha…what happened?" she breathed.

"Senior Don Juan and his lover were in bed together when Agatha caught them. She had the bullfighter's prized sword clutched in her hand and then…WHACK!!"

Dominic slapped his hands together, almost sending Anna through the roof.

"She thrust the sword into the ill-fated lovers, impaling the both of them. The sword went right through Senior de la Cruz and into the heart of the woman underneath him."

"Oh my *God*," Anna whispered. "What happened to Agatha?"

"I guess there was this big splashy trial and Agatha was sent to a mental institution for *twenty* years. Some say that when she was released, she was crazier than when she entered. Well, as soon as she was released she moved back in to this house...and what do you think she did?"

"I don't know," said Anna faintly.

"She went back to the scene of the crime, of course. This very room where you and I sit. You see, it was left untouched. The blood soaked bed was *still* there.

"Everything was *exactly* as it was twenty years before.

"Agatha could not bear another day without her bullfighter so she took a rope and hung herself on the chandelier that was above the deathbed. Katherine swears that she's seen the shadow of poor old Agatha swinging slowly in this room on several occasions. *I've* never seen it myself, but then again, I don't believe in spirits."

Anna stared at him in shocked silence. Her face was as white as a sheet.

Dominic faked a huge yawn. "I'm *beat*. All that talking really took it out of me, ya know? I think I'm gonna call it a night."

He stood up and started walking towards the door. "Goodnight, Anna. *Sweet* dreams," he purred.

Anna scrambled to her feet in a most unladylike fashion. "Wait! Don't go! I don't want to be in this creepy room. I want to be in *another* room! I don't care if it's a broom closet!"

Dominic put on a shocked face. "Why, Anna, surely you don't believe in ghosts?"

"No! Of *course* not!" she said indignantly. "It's just...I just..." she stopped talking abruptly.

Dominic's shoulders were shaking with laughter.

Anna sucked in a sharp breath, suddenly realizing she'd been had. "You made the whole thing up didn't you? Didn't you!" she yelled.

Dominic clutched his sides helplessly. He was laughing so hard he almost fell over. It was a deep resonant sound that echoed thought out the room.

Anna grabbed a pillow and flung it at his head. It bounced

harmlessly against his chest and landed with a soft plop at his feet.

It only made him laugh harder.

"How *could* you? You scared me half to death!" she cried.

Anna picked up two more pillows and hurled them at him. But, it was too much. His laughter was infectious. She started giggling despite herself. "I must admit, I *am* relieved. I had visions of crazy old Agatha swinging over my bed!"

Dominic wiped tears from his eyes and walked over to her. "Don't worry. The previous owners are happily retired in Europe somewhere."

"I'm glad to hear it!" She was almost faint with relief.

Dominic turned serious for a moment. "I hope I didn't scare you too much, Anna, I was just having a little fun. There's nothing for you to be afraid of here."

"I believe you," she whispered. And she did. He might be fearsome at times, but she knew that he would never harm her.

He moved closer to her until their bodies almost touched. If she were to move just slightly, she would be pressed against his chest. He tilted her chin up with his forefinger and simply stared at her. The only sound in the room was their breathing.

"I never told you how exquisite you look tonight, Anna. You are so *very* beautiful," he murmured.

He held her face in his hands and leaned down brushing his lips against hers. It was so soft and fleeting that Anna felt she'd only imagined it.

He softly traced her mouth with his velvety tongue. He stepped back and released her gently. "It's getting late, so I'll say goodnight. Thank you for sharing this evening with me."

"Goodnight, Dominic," said Anna huskily.

He smiled slightly and walked out of the room, closing the door quietly behind him.

Anna stood there for a while, lost in thought. She brought her fingers to her lips where she still felt the imprint of Dominic's.

She wished he had kissed her again. She wanted to taste his mouth and inhale his scent. She closed her eyes, swaying slightly.

She felt like she was sinking into a pool of quicksand. The more she fought, the faster she was going under, powerless to pull herself to solid ground. Everything was happening too fast.

She wasn't sure she could trust him, not yet anyway. And he certainly didn't trust her either. He had secrets. Old, *deep*, secrets that had yet to see the light of day. Anna had no doubts about that.

She was here for a purpose and Eric was the key to whatever reason she and Dominic had crossed paths.

Until they could trust each other, it seemed they would have to maintain their uneasy truce.

As Anna lay in bed, she resolved to gain Dominic's trust and respect. She smiled softly; tomorrow she would begin to try.

# Chapter Thirty-Three

"Dominic, you have a visitor."

Dominic looked up from his study at Katherine who was standing in the doorway. "Who is it, Kathy?" he asked distractedly.

"It's Miss *Rothchild*," said Katherine with a slight edge. *Davina*.

No wonder Katherine had that icy look. Davina had that effect on most people. Although she never said it, Dominic knew she disapproved of Davina Rothchild.

He sighed silently. "Okay, tell her I'll be out in a minute."

Katherine folded her hands in front of her. "Very well." She rolled her eyes to the heavens, muttering to herself as she left.

Davina was stretched languorously on his sofa when Dominic strode into the living room.

"Davina, what a surprise! I thought you were in Milan for the month." *And out of my hair.*

"Darling, you know me. I bore *so* easily; I couldn't take the same old parties with the same old people a minute longer. Besides," she rose and slinked towards him, pursing her full lips prettily. "I missed you *terribly*. Didn't you miss me too?" she asked coyly.

"Uh...yeah, sure I did." The truth was, he'd hardly spared more than a passing thought on her. All his energy was concentrated on Anna.

"You don't *sound* too convincing," she pouted.

She wrapped her arms around his neck, pressing her voluptuous body against his suggestively. "Prove it to me," she whispered.

She began kissing him ravenously, blissfully unaware that he wasn't returning the arduous kiss.

Anna hummed softly to herself as she made her way downstairs. She took special pains with her appearance. She had on a black wool wrap-around dress that softly molded itself to her curves. Boots in black suede completed the stylish look.

Her hair she left loose, hanging down her back in a shining curtain of silk. She felt beautiful and hoped Dominic appreciated the effort. She could not get the kiss they exchanged out of her head.

She heard soft murmuring coming from the living room and went in that direction. Dominic was in there. She felt her heart leap in her chest. She couldn't wait to see him.

Dominic was trying to extricate himself from the clinging arms of Davina when he heard a soft gasp.

He managed to gently push Davina off of him when he saw Anna framed in the doorway. Her face was pale, and he could see her rapidly blinking back tears. She was completely shocked and looked it.

Dominic silently cursed. Of all the bad timing, this one had to take the cake. He wiped his hand across his mouth and cleared his throat. He was uncharacteristically rattled.

"Anna! Good Morning. I…uh…I'd like to introduce you to Miss Davina Rothchild. She's an old friend," he explained quickly. "Davina, meet Anna Price. She'll be staying here for a while."

"Hello," Anna said faintly. "Nice to meet you."

Davina took her sweet time uncoiling herself from Dominic. The instant dislike was glaringly apparent in her icy green eyes. "Charmed," she said flatly.

She turned her attention back to Dominic, dismissing Anna entirely. "Sweetheart, I didn't know you were taking in boarders," she trilled annoyingly.

Only Davina could make a simple sentence sound rude and insulting. She ran her blood-red nails lightly down his cheek.

Dominic resisted the urge to jerk his face away from her. He recognized the dangerous glint in her eyes. She was furious and trying to cover it up. Davina seemed to think he was her personal property.

"Don't be ungracious, Davina, Anna is a guest in my home. Play nice," he said mildly. There was a thread of warning in his voice.

"Don't be so silly, Dominic. I was only *joking* for heaven's sake. I'm quite sure Miss…? What did you say your name was, dear?" she asked condescendingly.

Anna dug her fingernails into the soft part of her palms. Who did this carrot-topped, expensively dressed, harridan think she *was*?

She hated her and women just like her. Rich snobs who looked down their nose on everyone, and thought the whole world owed them because they were beautiful.

She set her chin and looked at her dead in the eye. "I didn't say. But, since you seem to be suffering from short-term memory loss, I'll tell you. It's Anna Price," she said icily.

*There. Take that and shove it, darling.*

"Why, you little *bitch*! Do you know who I *am*? I could by and sell you a thousand times over, I…"

"Davina! That's *enough*!" Dominic spun her around and glared at her. "I will not tolerate your rude behavior for another minute, do you understand? I want you to apologize to Anna right *now*."

Davina's face was flushed a most unflattering shade of red. "I will *not* apologize! *She's* the one with no breeding *and* no class. Really darling, I can't believe your consorting with this…this *person*. She's beneath you, and you know it."

Anna was trembling with fury. "Don't worry, he doesn't have to *consort* with me any longer. And as for *you*," she pointed a finger at Davina. "You might be beautiful on the outside. But what you have inside you is *rotten* and decayed. If this is how the upper class operate, then I'm glad I'm just a commoner." She turned and started walking out.

Dominic grabbed her arm. "Anna wait, I…"

She yanked her arm from his grasp. "Let me go!" Her eyes were blazing blue fire. "You failed to mention you had a girlfriend last night."

She stepped back and laughed harshly. "You're just like every other man. A lair and cheat with absolutely *no* honor."

Dominic jerked her to him. He was getting angry. "You don't

know what in the *hell* you're talking about."

"I know *all* too well, Dominic. Now let me go!" With Herculean effort, she pushed herself away from him. "You two *deserve* each other. You're cut from the same cloth!" She spun on her heel and stalked away.

Dominic ran his hands through his hair. "Shit!"

"Let her go, darling," said Davina. "She's not worthy of you." She stepped neatly in front of him. "Come on, Dominic. I've got the entire day blocked out for just the two of us. Why don't we go back to my place and spend the afternoon in bed."

Dominic looked down at her upturned face. Frankly, other than her being a decent attorney, he couldn't think of one redeeming quality she possessed.

He stepped away from her and looked at her for the first time. "I'm not gonna spend today or any other day with you, Davina. The thought of having sex with you turns my stomach.

"You're nothing but a spoiled, pampered *bitch*, and I've had enough of you to last me a lifetime."

"How *dare* you speak to me like that, you bastard!" Her face was ugly with malice. "I sure didn't hear any complaints from you when we were in bed together!"

"Yeah that's right, we both *used* each other. Don't pretend it was anything more than it was."

"As if I would," she sneered. "You're a lousy lay, Dominic, I've had much *better* than you."

Dominic laughed in her face. "I guess that wasn't you screaming like a bitch in heat when I made you come, huh, baby?"

Davina slapped him hard across his face. "You're a vulgar barbarian," she spat.

"So I've been told," he said in a bored tone.

"I don't know what I *ever* saw in you."

"My big cock. Now get the hell out of my house or I'll pick you up and *throw* you out," he rasped.

He took a step toward her. The look on his face must have convinced her he was serious because she snatched her purse and stormed out of the house, slamming the door behind her. Dominic gingerly rotated his jaw. Davina had some left hook.

He went into his study and pulled out a file. He strode out of the house, intent on finding Anna. She was most likely on the grounds somewhere.

He sighed in frustration. That woman was the most exasperating female on earth. She had gotten under his skin and there was nothing Dominic could do to stop it.

# Chapter Thirty-Four

Anna was completely lost. She had no idea how vast Dominic's estate was. She went running out the door without thinking it through. She had no money, no ID, not even a coat.

She shivered violently; it was a brisk forty degrees out. She was lost in the middle of Dominic's backyard, and she couldn't even find her way out. What a loser she was.

She resisted the urge to sit down and cry. She trudged on for what seemed like forever until she came to a clearing.

The grass here was perfectly maintained and lush. The place had a hushed, secretive aura to it. There was a reflecting pond where lily pads floated gently in the still waters. Beyond that, there was a small bench that sat in front of two graves.

Anna gasped softly. Strangely, she felt no fear. Only a sense of peace. She walked carefully over and sat down on the bench.

The gravestones were beautiful. Pale pink marble with intricately carved angles and cherubs adorned the markers. She leaned forward to read the inscriptions.

*ABIGAIL LOCKWOOD, BELOVED MOTHER.*
*JENNIFER MARIE LOCKWOOD, BELOVED SISTER.*
*SING WITH THE ANGELS.*

Anna was stunned. Poor Dominic…both his mother *and* his sister taken from him. She wondered how they had died.

And where was his father? Was he still alive? If not, then why wasn't he buried here?

Hmm…maybe he didn't have one. She didn't. She also lost her mother. They had much more in common then she realized. She reached out and touched the cold marble.

"What the *hell* are you doing here?"

Anna jumped up and saw Dominic sitting on top of his stallion. His voice was as cold as a gravedigger's. His face was closed and devoid of any emotion.

He dismounted and slowly walked towards her. His eyes were shuttered, and they pinned her like an insect to a card.

Anna was truly afraid. She had never seen him look as he did.

"I asked you a question. Answer me," he commanded.

"I...I...was lost," she stammered. "I couldn't find my way and...and...I just happened upon this place. So I sat down to rest..."

"You're trespassing. *No one* is allowed here," he said, cutting her off.

"I'm sorry! How was I to know that?" she cried.

"Well, now you know. You are *forbidden* here. Do you understand me?"

"Yes! I understand you! I'm not allowed in your precious sanctuary. I might *contaminate* it!" Anna was on the verge of tears. She was cold, tired, and hurt by his callous behavior.

"You're damn right about that," he said, his voice was like ice. He threw a file at her feet.

She bent down and picked it up. Her face lost what little color it had. "No," she whispered. "This *can't* be. No! This is a *lie*!"

Dominic laughed bitterly. "Pictures *never* lie, Anna, if that's your real name, which I seriously doubt.

"That's your mug shot and fingerprints. Along with a rap sheet a half-inch thick."

Anna shook her head in mute denial. Tears were running down her face.

"You and Eric made quite a team, didn't you? Scamming and deceiving innocent people.

"*Ruining* peoples lives, and for what? For *what*, Anna!" he shouted.

She wiped tears from her face. "Dominic, I don't know where you got this from but it's not me, I *swear* it! I've never gotten in to trouble in my life! Please, *believe* me!"

155

"How can I when you're lying? You're lying to me right now," he said tiredly.

"I'm not! I'm *not* Dominic! That woman might look like me, but it's *not* me! I could *never* hurt people like that, I'm not like Eric!" she sobbed. She dropped to her knees and held her face in her hands. "I'm not a bad person, I'm not…!" Anna was rocking back and forth on her knees, crying uncontrollably.

Dominic felt his heart break in two. He wanted so desperately to believe she was as innocent as she appeared. But, how could he? It was all there in black and white.

He walked over to her and scooped her up in his arms. "Let's go. It's cold, and you don't have a coat on," he said quietly.

She nodded in defeat. She cried herself out, and was now numb. They rode home silently.

As soon as they got in the house, Anna went straight to her room and closed the door. She was shivering as though she had palsy.

She ran a bath with water as hot as she could stand. Even submerged, she was chilled to the bone.

How could this have happened? Eric was behind it, she was sure of it. Hot angry tears ran down her cheeks. Would he *ever* stop ruining her life? What had she done to him to deserve this?

All she ever did was love him.

She leaned her head back and tried to think. She had to make Dominic understand that this was all a big mistake. This was Eric's doing, and she was going to prove it.

She jumped out of the tub and hurriedly dried herself off. She threw on a pair of jeans and a sweater. She had to talk to Dominic, make him see reason. She was innocent of any wrongdoing, and she wasn't going to stand still and have her reputation and her life maligned.

She searched the library and his study and couldn't find him. She went back upstairs and walked in the direction of his bedroom. The door was closed, as it always was, but she had a feeling he was in there. She licked her lips nervously and knocked softly on his door.

"Dominic? Are you in there? Can I speak to you, please?"

There was no answer. She put her hand on the doorknob, should she go in?

She was suddenly filled with trepidation. Her heart was beating like a drum. She turned the knob and entered his private domain.

His suite was entirely masculine. Colors in dark burgundy and navy complemented the heavy maple furniture. A huge four-poster bed dominated one corner of the large room. Braided rugs in burgundy, green and navy covered the wood floor. Leafy plants in Navajo pots gave the place a softer touch.

It was a beautiful room and Anna wished she could explore every inch of it. But she had to find Dominic. He obviously wasn't in here, so she needed to be on her way. As she turned to go, Anna paused, she could not resist the temptation to look.

She slowly walked over to his dresser. His wallet was lying there along with some spare change from his pocket. She smiled slightly, all men were the same in some ways. His hairbrush was there as well. It was a heavy silver one. Anna picked it up, turning it this way and that.

She ran it through her own hair. It was an erotic and forbidden thing to do. She placed it carefully on the dresser. She picked up a bottle of cologne and slowly unscrewed the cap. Breathing deeply, she brought it up to her nose. Her eyes closed involuntarily.

It was the same exotic scent he wore last night when he kissed her. Anna touched the top of the bottle with her finger and lightly rubbed some of the liquid on her neck. She smiled, remembering the feel of his lips upon hers.

She opened her eyes. Dominic was silently watching her.

She was frozen where she stood. Unable to move or even speak, the bottle of cologne was still in her guilty hands.

What must he think of her?

Dominic was naked from the waist up with only a pair of faded jeans on. The first two buttons were undone. They were soft and threadbare and fit him snugly.

Tiny water droplets beaded like crystals on his deeply muscled chest. His long hair was wet and attractively tangled around his face.

He'd just come out of the shower. Anna could smell the soap on him.

He stood motionless. His arms were loose at his sides and his expression was unreadable.

"Dominic…I…" Anna began.

"I came out to get my brush…I left it on the dresser," he said gruffly. His eyes glittered like silver pools.

Anna was mortified. She barged into his bedroom and rifled through his things. How could she be so *stupid* and thoughtless? No wonder he thought she was a criminal.

She carefully screwed the cap back on the bottle of scent and placed it where it belonged. "I knocked, but obviously you didn't hear me. That's no excuse for me to have entered your bedroom uninvited, Dominic. I truly apologize for my behavior," she stammered nervously.

She stood with her head bowed, embarrassed and unable to look him in the eye.

He slowly reached out and lifted her hand. He pressed it to the side of his face and closed his eyes. He was breathing rapidly as though he ran a marathon. He then placed it on top of his heart and opened his eyes.

They stood there for a time staring at each other. They could have been the only two people on earth.

There was only this room, this moment. Anna could feel the strong thudding of his heart beneath her hand.

"*Touch* me, Anna," he whispered with an ache.

She needed no more than that. Nothing else mattered.

Nothing.

She slowly ran her hands through his black hair, savoring the feel and texture of it. She brought a damp strand up to her nose and inhaled, smiling sensually as she did it.

With the lightest of touches, she delicately probed the planes of his face with her fingertips. They caressed silky eyebrows and tickled eyelashes. Anna traced the outline of his mouth gently, a slight smile on her lips.

He watched her quietly, thrilling at every touch. It was as light as a butterfly's wing. Her beautiful face was totally absorbed in what she was doing.

He caught one of her fingers between his teeth and nipped it softly.

She glided her hands down his chest slowly and leaned forward to softly kiss his heart.

With a sharp intake of breath, Dominic held her face in his hands and kissed her mouth. His tongue separated her lips, and, for the first time, he kissed her fully.

Her mouth was silky and warm, just as he imagined it would be. His tongue met hers and dueled lightly.

He lifted her heavy hair and pressed his open mouth against her neck. "*Anna*," he groaned.

He wanted her so badly. He never felt this all-consuming passion for any woman in his life. He was frightened by it. Frightened that he cared about someone above anything else, his work, his life, everything.

When did it happen?

How had this woman, his mortal enemy's wife, curled herself around his heart?

Anna ran her hands up and down his back, marveling at the silky smooth skin. Her tongue delicately licked the stray droplets of water on his chest. She pressed her lips against his nipple and lightly grazed it with her teeth. She felt a thrill run through her when she heard him groan softly.

She was completely lost in him. His scent, his taste, the feel of him against her body. She was falling in love with a stranger, and there wasn't a thing she could do to stop it. She might as well have stopped breathing.

Dominic lifted Anna effortlessly and crossed the room, depositing her gently on his bed. He stared down at her, his face intense with passion.

Anna felt boneless and lethargic, even lifting her hand seemed an impossible task. She licked her lips and softly spoke his name.

Dominic lowered himself on top of her and looked deeply into her eyes. "Are you sure?" he whispered hoarsely.

Lying on top of her was the sweetest agony. He wanted her so badly he was trembling, and he knew that once he had her, he'd never let her go.

Anna nodded. Every nerve in her body was alive and tingling. He was in her soul and in her blood.

He kissed his way down her smooth belly and circled his tongue around her navel. He unsnapped her jeans and hooked his fingers through the loops and tugged them off.

"Oh Dominic," she breathed. "*God...*"

He was depositing moist kisses along her pelvic bones and inner thighs. His warm breath on her was her undoing. She moaned and lifted her hips up slightly

He rubbed his chin against the soft core of her. "Say the words, Anna," he whispered urgently.

"I want you to make love to me, Dominic," she said huskily. Passion roughening her voice.

Breath hissed through Dominic's teeth as he lowered his head and kissed the delta between her legs. It was a deep, erotic soul kiss. "I don't care who you are, baby," he chanted sexily. "Because I want you so bad, I hurt. I want to touch every part of you. Be inside of you." He punctuated his words with light feathery kisses over her belly.

The sensual mist surrounding Anna slowly began to evaporate. He still thought she was a thief, a liar, and a con. "Dominic, stop...*please*, stop." She struggled to sit up.

Dominic looked at her with eyes still glazed with passion. "What? What is it, baby? Did I hurt you?" he asked with concern.

He was always conscious of his size and was careful that he wouldn't frighten or hurt a woman.

Anna shook her head. "No, Dominic, not in that way. It's just that...how can you say it doesn't matter who I *am*?

"It matters to me, and it should matter to *you* too. I'm not some slick hustler. I've never done anything illegal in my life."

"Anna please, let's not get into all of that," sighed Dominic. He swung up from the bed and ran his fingers through his hair impatiently.

"Can't we forget all of that for just a little while?" His voice lowered sensually. "I know you want me as badly as I want you."

"Don't change the subject," she said tremulously. She jerked on her pants and hurriedly snapped them up. "Do you believe that I could lie, cheat, and steal, Dominic? That I'm just a cheap little gold-digger with no morals whatsoever?"

His jaw hardened. *Dammit, why did she have to dredge her ugly past up for?*

"It's all there in black and white, Anna. You have a criminal record, I've *seen* it and so have you. I can't understand this need of yours to pretend otherwise."

"Then how could you stand to make love to me when you think I'm a such a lowlife?" she cried.

"Don't you think that the fact that *I do* makes me sick to my stomach?" he shouted.

The words reverberated through the room like a cannon blast.

Anna stared at him, shell-shocked. She rose from the bed with dignity, even though she was dying inside. Her heart felt like it would burst with shame.

"Anna! Wait...I...that didn't come out right..." Dominic grabbed her arm when she tried to go around him.

She wrenched her arm out of his grasp. "Don't bother giving me any phony excuses. You meant *exactly* what you said. You don't believe me, and you never will. From now on, keep your lousy hands off of me," she said icily.

Dominic's eyes narrowed. "Get out."

The words hung in the air, sibilant and deadly.

Anna spun on her heels and fled the room. Tears ran unchecked down her face as she ran into her suite. She flung herself on the bed and sobbed until she had no more tears left.

How could she have thrown herself at him like that? Her lack of self-control mortified her. He must have thought she was nothing but a tramp, a pathetically easy lay. He certainly didn't attach any sentimental feelings about what almost happened in his bedroom. She was a stupid fool to think that he actually cared about her. All he wanted was a physical release. He didn't respect her; he told her she made him sick to his stomach, didn't he? She made herself sick. How on *earth* would she face him again?

She sat up and slowly walked into the bathroom. She looked at herself in the mirror. It was a disheartening sight. Her face was splotchy and her nose was red as a cherry. She splashed cold water over her swollen eyes and dried her face. Only feeling marginally better, she flopped down on the small sofa that faced the ocean.

She needed to get her hands on that awful file Dominic showed her. Somewhere in there had to be some shred of evidence to prove she was innocent of any wrongdoing.

That woman at first glance might look like her, but it sure as hell *wasn't* her. There had to be slight differences in their facial structure to prove to Dominic that she was *not* the woman in that horrible photo. She shook her head in dismay. How could Eric have done this to her?

Somewhere deep inside her, a slow anger began to burn. "I will *not* give up," she whispered fiercely. "I'll make him believe me."

She stood up abruptly and with her head held high, went in search of the truth.

# Chapter Thirty-Five

**New York, The Bronx**

Eve Preston glared at Sheldon Leevy in utter disgust. He was hunched over her kitchen table eating cold chili straight from the can. The greasy, waxy orange sauce dribbled down his chin and onto his shirt. He didn't seem to notice or care.

It was nine o'clock in the morning.

"Jesus," she muttered, turning away before she threw up her morning corn flakes.

She stalked into her bedroom where Eric still lay sprawled across her bed snoring loudly, seemingly without a care in the world. The look she gave his inert form could have cracked the paint.

The both of them showed up at her apartment two nights ago. When she opened the door she almost screamed in fright. Before she could slam it in their faces, Eric said desperately, "Eve! Baby, it's *me*, Eric! I've come back!"

"*Eric?*" she said, squinting in amazement. Was this washed-out bum *really* Eric Robinson?

And if so, what on *earth* was he doing with the walking freak show? Eve planted a fist on her hip. Well one thing was for certain, she didn't back losers, and Eric Robinson had loser spelled out all over him.

"Come back to *what?*" she replied haughtily. "Not to *me*, Eric, I've moved on and I suggest you do the same." There was no way she was gonna let him freeload off of her.

Eric licked his lips nervously, "Come on, Eve," he wheedled. "Once you hear what I have to say, you'll be *beggin'* me for a piece of the action."

163

She viewed him skeptically. "I'm listening."

"Can we come in please, I'm sure you don't want your nosy neighbors listening to what I got to say."

Eve pursed her full lips. "You have *exactly* five minutes."

Five minutes turned into an hour, and then somehow before she knew it, Eric had persuaded her to let them stay for a while. A very *short* while, she stressed.

Having Eric here was bad enough, but having to put up with that troll in the next room was too much for any one person to have to bear.

"Wake up, Eric!" she snapped loudly. Giving the covers a vicious yank, she roughly shook him awake.

"Huh...? Wassamatter...?" Eric replied groggily.

"This is *not* a hotel," Eve said icily. "If you think I'm going to be catering to you and your friend, think again. Now kindly get *out* of my bed and in to a shower for God's sake, you stink to high heaven!"

"All right, all right," grumbled Eric sourly.

Jeez, nobody could accuse Eve of having the milk of human kindness running through her veins. She had ice water instead of blood. He stumbled into the shower and let the stinging spray pound his body until he felt remotely human.

God, it felt good to be back home in the States again. He would never again take his freedom for granted. The first thing he was gonna do was get a decent haircut, facial, and manicure. Then he'd get some clothes worthy of his magnificent body.

Cheered by the thought, he was humming as he toweled off and stood examining himself in front of the mirror.

Hmm...he'd seen some better days, but if he laid off the booze, the puffiness around his face would soon disappear. Thank the Lord his body was still relatively hard and muscled. The long tortuous days in prison kept him in shape. He was brown as a nut and his bloodshot green eyes glowed.

He chose to ignore the telltale signs of hard drinking and drugging that showed in his face. It looked markedly older. Fine wrinkles fanned at the corner of his eyes and mouth.

He was flexing his muscles when Eve flounced in. Eric turned around and surveyed her.

She was still a hot looking broad. Slim and cat-like, she exuded a sexual aura that was impossible to ignore. Her feral eyes held a thousand knowing secrets. Full scarlet lips were carnal and just a touch animalistic. Eric got a hard-on immediately and pulled her against him.

"How about it, Eve?" he whispered slyly. "It's been *sooo* long, and I want you so bad I can *taste* it." He laughed low-down and dirty at the double meaning. "Whaddaya say?"

"I say get a haircut and some new clothes and we'll see," replied Eve imperiously, disengaging herself from his cloying embrace. "In the meantime, I need to shower and *you've* got some shopping to do. So get out and take the freak with you." That being said, she ushered him out of the bathroom and firmly shut the door in his face.

"Hey, how about floating me a small loan, just until we hit the mother lode? Huh…? Eve…?" He tapped on the door.

"I'm not a bank, Eric, so forget it. Ask your new best friend, otherwise you're shit out of luck," she called.

He heard the shower water running and cursing viciously, he kicked her nightstand, painfully stubbing his toe in the process. He threw on an old pair of Levis and tee shirt he'd left in her closet, and then limped into the kitchen where Sheldon was slurping down the last of his breakfast.

Eve was right about one thing; Leevy was a walking horror show. His frizzy hair was a greasy mess, but that was nothing compared to his jacked-up face and insane floating eye.

"Hiya, Eric," he said cheerfully. "How's it hangin'?"

He tipped his head in the direction of the bedroom. "Man, oh, man, she is one *hot* number," he smacked his oily lips together and grinned. "Didja get lucky?"

His teeth looked like they'd never seen a toothbrush in his life. The chili was stuck between his upper incisors, and the view wasn't pleasant.

Eric shuddered in disgust. He couldn't wait until Sheldon outlived his usefulness. Until then he'd have to put up with his filthy habits. "What me an' Eve do is none of *your* business," he snapped. "You'd better watch yourself around her, Sheldon. One wrong move and she'll use your balls for fish bait. And that's after I rip em' off. You catch my drift?"

Sheldon bobbed his head. "Sure, Eric, I didn't mean no disrespect, honest. She's quite a looker is all I meant. I'll be no trouble, I swear."

"Yeah, no problem," said Eric.

He casually walked to the fridge and pulled out a carton of orange juice. Pouring himself a glass, he sat down next to Sheldon. He had to play this right. "Uh, Sheldon…if we're gonna put this plan into motion, I'm going to have to dress the part. I mean I can hardly wear the rags I came here in. Know what I mean?"

Leevy stared at him dumbly.

Eric gritted his teeth and tried another tack. "I need some up-front money, a coupla thousand or so ought to do it."

"A coupla *thousand* dollars! Jeez, I dunno, Eric, that's a buncha money. I mean I paid the bus fare to get us here an' all. Can't your…uh…*friend* Eve give it to you?"

Eric's first instinct was to grab the nearest knife and slit the ungrateful fucker's throat from ear to ear. He actually cut his eyes toward a cutlery set resting on the counter, but unfortunately, he still needed him.

"No, I can't borrow it from Eve, Sheldon. She's in a bit of a cash crunch right now. Look, this is a temporary loan. I mean we're only talkin' a couple of days. You'll have twenty times that amount, I promise you. Unless you want out. But then you'll have to clear outta here like *now*, buddy. Eve doesn't put up with freeloaders. It's too bad really, we coulda made a great team…" Eric let his voice trail off sadly.

"No, no, Eric! I still want *in* this deal. I'll lend you the money, no problem. The amount just caught me off guard." Sheldon's eye was floating crazily in its socket.

Eric was the only friend he'd ever had. He still had five grand stashed in a money belt around his waist. Two thousand dollars was a small price to pay to finally get even with Dominic Lockwood.

Eric's eyes glittered like an animal's. Everything was falling into place just as he'd planned. "That's excellent, Sheldon, really good." He clapped him on the shoulder with an excited whoop. "Well, come on, boy! We got some shopping to do."

**\*\*\*\*\*\*\*\*\*\***

A few of hours later, Eric strutted out of the expensive salon feeling like a million bucks. His blond hair was freshly cut and perfectly styled. It gleamed with health and vitality. The facial did wonders for him as well. His skin was soft and glowing.

He paused to adore his image in a storefront window. The tailored brown slacks and turtleneck he wore complemented his coloring perfectly. As did the brown suede coat he wore over them. The new clothes felt sensuous against his skin. He looked like a high-priced gigolo.

A lovely brunette strolled by and flirtatiously smiled at Eric.

"Howz' it goin', sweetheart?" he crooned with a dazzling smile.

She giggled lightly as she passed, her lush hips swinging rhythmically underneath a tight skirt.

Ahh…to be back in the game *and* in top form felt wonderful.

A black Chevy van pulled smoothly up to the curb. Eric sent Sheldon, who was lumbered down like a pack-mule with all Eric's purchases, to rent a car. He pulled open the door and slid in.

"*Wow*, Eric, you look like a friggin' movie star!" Sheldon exclaimed.

Eric flipped down the mirrored visor and checked out his image, yet again. "Yeah I do, don't I?" he said cockily.

"Where to now?" Sheldon wanted to know.

"Back to Eve's."

Eric let himself quietly into Eve's bedroom. He had sent Sheldon on some meaningless errands just to get him out of the apartment for an hour or so. She had her back to him; she was fastening on a pair of diamond earrings. He crept up and spun her around, pushing her against the wall.

"Do I meet with your approval *now*, Miss Eve Preston?" he whispered. There was a thread of violence in his tone. He was gonna make her pay for her slight earlier that morning.

She tilted her head up at him, her sly eyes taking in his new transformed image. "It's quite an improvement." She ran her tongue over her moist lips in a way she knew would get his juices flowing.

He yanked her blouse open sending pearl buttons flying.

"You lousy son of a bitch." She slapped him hard across his face. Her eyes shone with sexual heat.

Eric slapped her back and grabbed a handful of her hair, bringing her face close to his. "God, I've missed you," he growled.

He kissed her hard, while pulling off her blouse and skirt. She never wore any underwear, so he had full access. They made their way to the bed with a maximum of groaning, kissing, and biting.

Eve undressed him in a matter of seconds, trailing her pointed tongue all over his body like a snake. He grunted and pushed her to her knees, and Eve went willingly.

Eric was about to come in to a shitload of money, and she was going to be right there with him. Money and power were the only things that totally turned her on.

Eric hauled her to her feet and tossed her on the bed, flipping her onto her tummy. He entered her with a warrior's yell. And together they came, bucking and writhing all the way.

Sweat-soaked and gasping, they lay entwined. The both of them were two sides of the same dark coin.

They began to make their plans....

# Chapter Thirty-Six

**The Hamptons**

Dominic slowly walked into his study. Anna was seated behind the massive desk, poring over the infamous file. She must have been there the entire night because she had the same clothes on.

She was so engrossed in what she was doing she didn't even hear him enter the room. He stood there for a moment watching her. She was so very lovely.

He cleared his throat. She looked up at him and gravely watched as he approached her.

"I suppose you're wondering why I'm in your private domain?" Anna laughed self-depreciatingly, "I seem to be doing an awful lot of that lately."

"I can see that you're looking at your criminal record."

"Not mine, no," she countered. "Whoever this woman is, it's not me. Just take a closer look at this mug-shot, Dominic." She pulled the black and white photo out of the folder and laid it on top of the desk.

"Her eyes are a little smaller than mine are. And the shape of her nose and mouth are similar to mine, but not *exactly* so. My nose is straighter. Hers is a tiny bit longer. My upper lip is thinner than my bottom. Both her lips are full. Her hair is straight, mine's wavy. Look at her eyebrows; they're not high and arched. Mine are. It's not *me*, Dominic. If you really study the picture, you'll see."

He looked at her upturned face. It was honest and open. God, he wanted to believe her so badly. He took the photo and sat on the edge of the desk. He studied the woman in the picture carefully. At first glance he would have sworn it was Anna, but if you took in to consideration all the little differences Anna stated, then yes, there was a difference. It was slight here and there, but it *was* different.

His heart leapt in his chest. *Maybe, just maybe...*

Anna sensed his confusion and scrambled out of her chair. "Do you believe me, Dominic? Please say you're starting to *believe* me!"

He slowly raised his head and stared deeply into her eyes. He was afraid and unsure of himself for the first time in years.

Hope.

He'd forgotten what it felt like. "I want to Anna," he whispered with an ache. "I really want to."

Twin tears formed in his eyes and slid down his cheeks. He squeezed his eyes shut and turned around, trying to get himself under control.

Anna was stunned. Dominic was a man who *never* showed his emotions. She knew how much it cost him, showing this side of himself to her. She gently turned him around and cupped his beautiful face in her hands.

"Dominic," she whispered. "I swear on everything I hold dear to me that I'm telling you the truth. I don't know how Eric managed to replace this woman's fingerprints with mine, but somehow he *did* it. All those crimes, those are *her* crimes, *her* sins...not mine."

Dominic pressed his face against her palm. "I've been alone for a lot of years, Anna. That's all I know. It's all I've ever counted on. I...I'm..." He shrugged his shoulders helplessly. "I'm afraid of trust and of love...of *loving*. Does that make any sense?"

She nodded, "Yes, Dominic, it does." She smiled a sad, understanding smile that was a thousand years old. "I know what it's like to be truly alone, I *know* what real loneliness can do to you. We're more alike than even we know."

Dominic pulled her against him and kissed her mouth. It was the sweetest, most gentle kiss she'd ever experienced in her life. "You don't ever have to be alone again," he whispered.

He took her hand and led her in front of the fireplace. Simultaneously, they sank to their knees. They were only a breath apart. With hands barely touching, they traced each other's faces, and for the first time, it was just Dominic and Anna.

He slowly unbuttoned her sweater and slid it off her shoulders. Dominic gazed in wonder at the satiny perfection of her breasts. He pressed his open mouth against her skin. Anna let out a sigh that sounded more like a breeze. He pulled his shirt off and grazed her nipples with his chest over and over again, until they were hard and aching.

He placed his large hands behind her back and traced light little circles up and down her spine. Dominic bent his head and drew her nipple in his mouth, brushing it back and forth with his tongue. He softly bit and smiled when she moaned his name.

Anna couldn't take it any more. She wrapped her arms around him and kissed him with all the love and yearning she had trapped inside her. Dominic was white-hot and out of control with desire. He groaned and pushed her onto the carpet. He stripped off her jeans and hooked his thumbs into the waistband of her silk underwear. He slowly slid them down her legs until she lay naked before him.

His chest was rapidly rising and falling. "My God," he breathed in awe. Her beauty humbled him. She surpassed anything he'd ever imagined or hoped for.

He rose gracefully to his feet and removed the rest of his clothes. His eyes never left her face.

They burned, *burned* into hers.

Anna swallowed dry-mouthed. He was Michaelangelo's *David*. Magnificently proportioned in every way. He personified male beauty. And she was so lucky this beautiful, complex man saw something in her that no one else had seen before.

She held out her hand to him, and he knelt in front of her, kissing the palm and each of her fingers. She sat up and traced the contours of his chest and ribcage with her tongue until he trembled. Anna shyly kissed his navel, and lower until she came to the most tantalizing part of him. She softly licked the underside of his penis and circled the head until a tiny drop of moisture beaded the tip.

"Baby, you're killing me," he gasped.

He gently laid her down and blazed a trail of wet, open-mouthed kisses from her collarbone, to her breasts and down her stomach. He parted her legs and dipped his tongue into her. He circled the small seed of flesh, kissing and gently biting until Anna thought she'd lose her mind from the sheer ecstasy of it.

"Dominic," she cried helplessly, thrashing her head from side to side.

He looked up and smiled tenderly. "Shh...I know, sweetheart. I'll get you there, I will," he whispered erotically. He sat up and with his knee parted her legs and entered her in one smooth thrust. "Oh *God*," he moaned. "You're so sweet, baby. So *sexy* and exciting."

He held her face between his hands and kissed her deeply, thrusting his tongue in her mouth, mating it with hers.

He thought this is what heaven must be like.

He wanted to stay inside Anna forever. He loved her, would always love her until the day he died.

Anna was spinning wildly out of control.

She thought this is what true and utter joy is.

He filled her in body, and in her heart and soul as well. Her love for him was complete and final. She would love him until she drew her last breath.

She could feel the exquisite feeling building inside her like a thousand butterflies waiting to be freed. She moaned frantically.

"Yes, Anna...come with me. I want to watch you come," he whispered urgently.

He laced his fingers through her hair, and watched, spellbound, as she climaxed. She made sexy little noises at the back of her throat "Oh, Dominic, *Ohh*..." she moaned sensually, her back beautifully arched.

It was his undoing; he began to move inside her and came in a series of long, shuddering spasms.

Much later, they lay entwined, and he told her all about his painful childhood. He told her about the physical and emotional damage his father had done to his wife and children and what is was like growing up desperately poor.

He nearly broke down when he spoke of his mother's suicide and the responsibility that was placed on his young shoulders because of it. Then finally, he told her all about Jenny and what happened to her. But, not Eric's part in it. He couldn't tell her, not yet. Eric was out there somewhere, waiting like a spider to make his move.

Anna cried quietly while listening to him. She couldn't imagine how hard his life had been. She felt ashamed that she taunted him about his silver-spoon life of luxury.

If she had only known.

Her heart went out to his sister, as well. God, the poor girl had been callously used and then thrown away like a piece of trash. What kind of a man would *do* that?

Dominic was right; this person *was* responsible for Jenny's tragic death. It was a shame that he never found out the identity of the man.

Haltingly, she told him about her life and the pain of losing her mother. Of Eric and their horrible marriage. The years of being the sole breadwinner working sometimes two jobs, while he spent the money as fast as she could earn it.

How he physically abused her and cheated on her. The sneaky way he'd squandered her mother's legacy. His drug and alcohol habit. And finally, the trouble he'd gotten them into by his gambling debts. All of it.

Dominic's face was a tight, angry mask. That motherfucker was gonna *pay* with his life. The thought of him beating Anna filled him with an out-of-control rage. It made him sick to think of how that scum implicated Anna in this whole mess.

He obviously was screwing the whore whose picture was in that mug shot. He had *no doubt* that Anna was not the woman he thought she was. She couldn't have made love to him like that, with her whole heart and soul and be a decayed inside.

No way.

Eric somehow found a dead ringer for Anna. And together they conspired to use her for God knows what.

He had to tread very carefully from here on out. Until things neutralized, Anna was in danger, and that was unacceptable. He hated keeping secrets from her, but that's how it had to be. When it was all over, he'd tell Anna everything. He wouldn't hold anything back. Then they'd have the rest of their lives to love each other without Eric's dark shadow standing between them.

He smiled at her. "You know what?" he asked softly.

"What?"

"We've wasted too much time talking about Eric, he's nothing. I want you to put him out of your mind, Anna. He'll never hurt you again, not while I'm on this earth. I swear it to you."

He stated it simply as a fact, and Anna believed him unequivocally. Her eyes darkened with passion. She combed her fingers through the soft hair on his chest and glided her hand down to gently squeeze his long, thick shaft. "I believe you. *And* I agree with you." She softly kissed his upper jaw, licking and nibbling her way to his lips. "We've wasted *way* too much time talking."

He groaned and kissed her. Anna was a very smart woman.

*********

The sun rose like a pat of melting butter, all soft and golden, and warm. It gently lit the darkened room and cast a honeyed glow over them both. Dominic awoke and gazed at Anna's beautiful face. It was clear and peaceful. Her blue-black hair was spread out over the pillow like a cloud. He softly kissed her lips.

He never knew how wonderful it could feel to wake up next to someone you loved. He had made a rule for himself, he never spent the whole night with a woman.

Usually after sex, he was ready to ease himself out of whatever bed he found himself in. A task that was never easy because the woman would almost always be pissed off about it.

Dominic couldn't help it. Once the sex was over, he felt lonely and empty inside. All it was to him was a physical release and nothing more. There were many that thought they could change him, but quickly learned when he froze them out. He never did it in cruel way, but it was final nonetheless.

Now, looking at Anna, he felt hopeful and almost carefree. Like he wasn't meant to travel his life alone and lonely. He could dream of a future like normal people did. He gently traced her face. She'd make a wonderful mother. Soft and loving, like his mom was. Like Jenny would have been, had she lived.

Dominic carefully got up. He needed to shower and get to his Manhattan office. He was meeting with Nick Rossi this morning, and he had a lot to tell him.

He quickly scribbled a note and plucked a red rose from a crystal vase on the desk and gently laid it next to her head. Dominic silently left the study where Anna was sleeping without a care in the world.

# Chapter Thirty-Seven

"Mr. Lockwood? Inspector Rossi is here."

"Thanks, Bea. Send him in."

Inspector Nick Rossi strolled in looking the very epitome of Italian *GQ*. He was exquisitely dressed, as always. Tall, dark and athletic, women flung themselves at him on a regular basis. Even his secretary, the frosty Ms. Bea, twittered like a schoolgirl around him.

His curly brown hair fell boyishly around his matinee-idol face. Chocolate-colored almond eyes surrounded by a forest of long lashes twinkled most attractively. And if that wasn't the kicker, he had dimples on either side of his sensual mouth.

Dominic smiled at his only and best friend. "I think Bea is hot for you," he joked.

Nick flopped down on the easy chair. "Yeah?" He grinned. "I wonder what it's like with an older woman."

"You're a fuckin' pervert, Rossi, she's at least sixty-five!"

"Hey, don't knock it till you've tried it, my man. She'd probably be *real* grateful."

"God, is there anyone safe from your dubious charms?"

Nick displayed his pearly white teeth in a dazzling smile. "I *seriously* doubt it," he said smugly.

Dominic chuckled and poured the both of them cups of hot, fragrant coffee.

Nick blew on his and turned serious. "So…heard anything from our friend?"

"No, not yet. And I'm worried, Nick. I thought by now he'd have made his move."

"Don't worry. He'll turn up. You've got his woman and he'll be wantin' her back."

"I'll rip him apart if he lays a hand on Anna." Dominic's face tightened with fury.

Nick looked at him flabbergasted. "Hey…what's goin' *on*? Don't tell me you're *falling* for this broad, Dominic?" said Rossi totally surprised. "She's got a sheet longer than my dick."

"No, she doesn't, Nick. Look…it's a long story, but believe me, Anna Price is completely *innocent* of any wrongdoing."

"How can you be so sure?" Nick wanted to know.

"I just am. The woman in that mug shot is *not* Anna. Somehow that prick Robinson found an Anna lookalike. Go figure, right? Anyway, it's *her* rap sheet. They must have drugged Anna and switched fingerprints. Trust me, Nick, Anna's a *good* woman. Her only mistake was marrying Eric."

Nick assessed his friend shrewdly. "Huh…I never thought I'd see the day."

"What?" said Dominic irritably.

"I never thought I'd see you fall in love. And you are, aren't you? Head over heels by the looks of it," he crowed.

Dominic leaped out of his chair and prowled his office restlessly. "You don't know what you're talkin' about," he muttered lamely.

"Ha! My *ass*! Look at you…you're totally *pathetic*! Jesus, this Anna must be *some* woman."

"She *is* Nicky. She's pure and trusting and God, she's so incredibly beautiful. Just being with her makes me feel clean inside. And I haven't felt like that in…I don't know *how* long. That's why I gotta resolve this thing quickly."

Nick nodded. "You got me. You know you can count on me when the time comes."

"C'mon, Rossi, you know I can't let you do that. Christ, you're a *cop*…"

"That's *Inspector*, thank you very much, and *I* know where to draw the line. We go back way too many years for me to puss out on you now. You know how to reach me."

Dominic stared at his friend. A better man you'd never find. "Thanks, man," he said gruffly.

"Hey." Nick hugged him and clapped him on the back. "You can't have *all* the fun."

He picked up his cashmere coat and strode out of the office, pausing to flirt a little with Ms. Bea.

Dominic shook his head in amusement. The man had no shame.

# Chapter Thirty-Eight

Sheldon Leevy hunkered down between the hedges surrounding Lockwood's mansion in the Hamptons.

*Some people had all the luck,* he thought bitterly.

That fucker Lockwood sure had some set-up goin'. A fancy house, cars, servants, and lots of money. While he, Sheldon Leevy had squat. Well, that was gonna change soon enough. Yessiree, he and Eric had it all figured out.

He spied the older man outside directing the gardeners where to prune and mow. They were right on schedule. He and Eric had been casing the place out for a few days and the servants always stuck to the same schedule. He knew how to get in. The trick was not getting caught.

He ducked down when the old man passed by. He waited a minute until he saw him disappear into the house. He hopped over the hedge and pulled out a baseball cap he had in the back pocket of his workman's overalls. He shoved it on his head and walked quickly towards the main house with his chin buried in his chest. If anybody saw his face, it'd be all over.

He made his way into the mudroom behind the kitchen without incident. Now was the difficult part. He clutched the nine-millimeter pistol in his hand and silently made his way through the kitchen. Nobody had better get in his way. If they did, well...killing never bothered him in the slightest.

**\*\*\*\*\*\*\*\*\***

Anna stepped out of the shower with a soft smile on her face.

The events of the previous night were burned into her memory. She blushed hotly when she remembered their fiery lovemaking. Dominic was a superb lover, passionate, intense, tender and giving.

She briskly dried herself and belted a satin robe around her waist. Dominic would be home in time for lunch, and she wanted to look beautiful for him.

She *felt* beautiful…and light, and trouble-free for the first time in years. She was humming to herself when she entered the bedroom. She stopped short when a man pointing a gun straight at her was lounging on her bed.

"Well, howdy, Anna. You don't know me," Sheldon slid his tongue over his wet lips obscenely. "But we both have a mutual friend, and he sent me to come get you. You remember, Eric, doncha? Your *husband*?"

Anna's eyes were dilated in shock. The man before her looked like a monster. He was hideously disfigured, but more than that, he looked evil. Totally and completely evil.

Too terrified to even scream, Anna stood rooted to the floor.

Sheldon sat up and looked over his shoulder nervously. "Don't you go gettin' any cute ideas about screamin' or carryin' on, ya hear?" He waved the gun wildly. "Or I'll blow you *away*…understand?"

Anna forced herself to remain calm. "Please. Don't hurt me okay? I promise I'll do as you say." *Oh Dominic, where are you?*

Sheldon flicked his limp hair out of his eyes. "Damn straight you will." Never taking his eyes off her, he pulled open the closet door and yanked a pair of slacks and sweater off their hanger. "Get dressed." He threw the clothes at her feet. "You and I are gonna walk outta here real nice and easy. If you try and scream for help I swear I'll start shootin' up the joint."

She nodded while picking up the clothes and hurried to the bathroom. Sheldon ran in front of the bathroom door blocking her way. "You'll get dressed in front of *me*," he said thickly. He was sweating profusely, and his eyes slid down her body like slime.

Anna was trembling with fury. "Go to hell."

Sheldon slapped her hard across her face. "Look, bitch. Either you put your clothes, on or I *will*." He wagged his tongue in front of her face. "I know *I'd* enjoy it."

She licked the blood from the side of her mouth and quickly began dressing. Sheldon began rubbing his erection through his pants. "Yeah…man, you are sooo *sweet*," he grunted.

Anna shuddered in fear and revulsion as he masturbated in front of her.

After he gratified himself, he pulled a cell phone out of his pocket and tossed it to her. "Before we leave, you're gonna make a phone call and if you do *exactly* as I tell you, your boyfriend Lockwood won't die. Got it?"

"What have you done with Dominic?"

"Nothing. *Yet*. But that'll change in a heartbeat if you make one stupid move. Do I make myself clear?"

"Yes," she whispered. "I'll do exactly as you say. Only please, *please* don't hurt him."

Sheldon snickered nastily. "Ain't love grand."

**\*\*\*\*\*\*\*\*\*\***

Dominic grabbed his car keys from the desk and turned to leave his when his private line rang. "Hello?"

"Dominic?"

"Anna?" he smiled, surprised. "Hey, I was just about to leave the city. I'll be home in a couple of hours. I can't wait to see you," he whispered softly.

Anna's throat ached with unshed tears. Her heart was breaking in little pieces. She forced a smile into her voice. "You won't have to wait that long," she said lightly. "I'm actually across the street at a pay phone. It's in front of O'Shaunessy's Deli."

"Yeah, I know. I go there all the time." Dominic went very still.

Anna didn't know where his office was. *Who the hell brought her here?* "How did you get here, Anna?" Alarm bells began going off in his head.

"I…I…I don't know how to say this except just to say it. Eric brought me here, Dominic."

"What the *hell* are you talking about?" His voice was deadly quiet.

"He's changed, Dominic, he really has. He...he...wants another chance, and I'm thinking of going back to him." Tears were rolling down her face. "Please, *please* forgive me. I wouldn't *hurt* you for anything in the world." Her voice ended on a sob.

"You're a Goddamn liar," he whispered. "Don't try and tell me what we have isn't *real*, Anna. This is a bunch of bullshit."

"I...I'll tell you to your face if you don't believe me, Dominic. We'll be waiting across the street." Anna put the phone down and began shaking as if she had palsy.

"Very touching," Sheldon sneered. "C'mon, we gotta go." He grabbed her by the upper arm.

# Chapter Thirty-Nine

Dominic ripped the phone from the wall and threw it across the room. He punched a cantaloupe-sized hole in the wall of his office and stalked by a stunned Ms. Bea. Too impatient to wait for the elevator, he yanked open the door to the stairs, slamming it behind him.

His feet were a blur; it was just a continuous rat-a-tat of his shoes hitting the stairs. He was in a blind and killing rage. Robinson was gonna die today. It was long overdue.

He burst out of the building like a madman. He quickly scanned the street directly across from him and sure enough, there was Anna and Eric. Robinson indolently waved at him and then with a smirk, pulled Anna to him, kissing her passionately. His hands were roaming all over her body.

Dominic staggered back as if he'd been shot. All the breath left his body in one painful hiss. A black curtain fell in front of his eyes and like a robot, he crossed the street unaware of anything but his mortal enemy.

Eric pushed Anna away from him so she had her back to Dominic. He had a smug smile on his face and stood with his legs spread apart in an arrogant stance. "C'mon, motherfucker," he taunted. "Let's see what you got."

Dominic crossed the space between them with astonishing speed. His hands were up around his face like a boxer. He was ready for him. As soon as his foot touched the curb, Eric quickly stepped back and around him. He hopped into a black Chevy van parked on the street and gunned the engine.

Anna stepped smartly in front of him. Only, it wasn't Anna. It looked like her from a distance, but up close there was only a passing resemblance. His face registered surprise, then dread. *Fuck! He'd been set-up!*

This was a hard-looking and bitter woman. Her pinched face was over-made up and sly. Cold blue eyes glittered up at him. "Well, well," she purred. "Eric didn't tell me you were such a *big*, handsome man."

She squeezed his cock lightly. With her other hand, she brought a Taser up and jolted Dominic in the solar plexus. He grunted as his body received the shock. He slumped on top of Eve who staggered under his weight.

Eric slid open the side-door of the van, and Eve quickly shoved him in. They took off and sped into the noon traffic.

# *Chapter Forty*

Sheldon pushed Anna into the empty warehouse. She nearly fell, but she managed to stay on her feet. He pointed to a battered wood chair. "You sit still and shut up."

He punched out a number on his cell phone. "Yeah, it's me. I got her. Uh-huh. No," he scoffed. "She ain't gonna give me *no* trouble. I gar-*run*-tee it." His laugh was evil. "I'll see ya soon."

He sauntered over to her and whispered in her ear. "Soon we're gonna have ourselves a *real* party. Take your clothes off." He licked her ear and snickered dirtily.

His fetid breath made Anna want to gag, but she kept her face expressionless. He wanted a reaction and she was dammed if he was going to get one. All she could do was wait like a lamb to slaughter. She prayed that Dominic was safe. But in her heart she knew that wasn't the case.

**\*\*\*\*\*\*\*\*\***

Dominic regained consciousness just as they were pulling into the warehouse. He slowly opened his eyes and looked up slightly. Eric and the woman were in the front of the van talking quietly. Dominic couldn't make out what they were saying.

A metal screen separated him from the both of them. His stomach felt bruised and tender. He gingerly touched his ribs, wincing in pain, and carefully lifted his shirt. There were two small burn marks up high on his stomach, right between his ribcage.

*Son-of-a-bitch! She shocked me with a fuckin' Taser!*

He felt around his pockets for his cell phone. "Shit," he muttered.

He remembered he left it on his desk. He frowned, feeling an unfamiliar object in his coat pocket. He pulled out a small metal box with a toggle switch on it. He turned on the switch and a red light began flashing. He smiled.

Rossi.

He must have slipped the homing device in his pocket this morning. He prayed to God his friend would come through for him in time. The van jerked to a stop. He heard them getting out. Dominic closed his eyes and waited.

Eric pulled the side-door open and peered inside. He had a silver Magnum .357 gripped in his hand. He glanced at Eve. "He's still out cold."

He began banging the gun against the metal doorframe. "Hey, asshole! Rise and shine!"

Dominic gritted his teeth in fury. It went against everything he stood for not to come out swinging. Instead, he slowly rose and stepped out of the van and into the dark warehouse.

His eyes were on Eric, fixed and staring. The hatred in them was almost palatable. He rose to his full height of six foot six and flexed his muscles threateningly. "Why don't you put the gun down? Huh, Eric? Too much of a *pussy*? C'mon, Motherfucker...let's go," he growled.

Eric was glad for the gun. Lockwood looked like a stone-cold killer, but this time *he* had the upper hand. "Nice try," he sneered. "You think I'm fuckin' *stupid*? Face it, Lockwood, I set your dumb ass *up* and you're gonna pay for every agony you put me through. This time, *I'm* your judge, jury and executioner. I'm gonna make you wish you were never born."

"I seriously doubt it. Today is the last day you'll spend on this earth, Robinson. I *promise* you." Dominic glared at him.

"*Oooh,* did you hear that, Eve? I'm so fuckin' *scared*, I'm gonna wet myself," he snickered.

Eve smoked a cigarette and looked bored. "Enough with the macho bullshit, Eric. Let's get this over with." She blew a solid stream of smoke through her nostrils.

Eric threw a pair of handcuffs at Dominic. "Put these on."

"Why don't you come over here and put them on me yourself," Dominic whispered.

Eric's right eye twitched spasmodically. "Eve!" he yelled. "Go and cuff him."

Dominic bared his white teeth in a frightening smile. "Yeah, Eve, why don't you come on over."

"Shut the fuck up!" Eric screamed.

Eve looked at Dominic with feral eyes. "You don't think I *won't*?"

She slowly walked towards him. Her lush hips were swaying underneath a tight, short skirt. She stopped a few inches in front of Dominic. She carefully knelt down in front of him and picked up the cuffs.

"Careful, Eve," warned Eric. He glared at Dominic and brought the gun up. "You make *one* move and I'll punch a hole between your eyes."

Eve rose seductively, rubbing her body against his all the way up. The sexual heat in her eyes was animalistic. "Put your hands out," she whispered, licking his lips like a cat.

In one swift move, Dominic spun her around so she was in front of him. His forearm was a steel band across her throat. "Put the fuckin' gun down or I'll snap her neck, Eric. *Do* it!" he shouted.

Eric threw his head back and laughed. "You think so, huh? Well guess *what*, Dominic? I've got a little surprise for you. Well, *two* really, but I'm getting ahead of myself." He turned. "Hey, Sheldon, hit the lights."

The fluorescent tubes overhead suddenly came on, flooding the place with harsh light.

There in the middle of the room was Anna, gagged and bound to a chair with nothing on but her silk bra and underwear. Her eyes were filled with tears. She made small whimpering sounds when she saw Dominic.

"*AANNAA!*" Dominic screamed.

Eric smiled triumphantly. "I suggest you let Eve go, that is if you want your precious Anna to live."

Dominic slowly let her go. She turned around and slapped him in the face. "Asshole!" she spat.

"You're a fuckin' *dead* man, Robinson," his voice shook with intensity.

"So you keep saying, Dominic," replied Eric drolly. "But I wouldn't count on it if I were you. There's one more person I'd like you meet. Well, actually you met him a *long* time ago. But I know you'll recognize his face." Eric was alive with malice and ill will.

A tall, skinny man appeared. He was frightening to look at. The right side of his face was scarred and puckered. Sheldon Leevy looked at Dominic with a nasty smile. "Well, lookey here, if it ain't the great Dominic Lockwood. Not so high and mighty now, are you?"

# Chapter Forty-One

Dominic lunged toward his sister's murderer with a roar. At the same time, Eve came up from behind him with a long piece of rebar. Swinging it like a bat, she struck the side of his head. Dominic fell to his knees, momentarily stunned. Blood was pouring from an ugly gash on the side of his forehead.

Eric ran to Anna, who was screaming hysterically. He wrapped his fist around her hair and jerked her head up. He put the gun to her temple. "One more stupid move and I'll blow her head off, Lockwood, I *swear* I will!"

Dominic felt dizzy and nauseous. Drawing a shaky breath, he said, "Why don't you let Anna go? It's me you want, not her."

"Oh, I can't do that, Dominic," he replied with false sincerity. "Much as I'd like to, I just *can't*. You see, Anna here is gonna help me get a whole *lotta* money. Ain'tcha, baby-cakes?"

He removed her gag and kissed her hard, shoving his tongue into her mouth. She moaned frantically, twisting her head away from him.

"Leave her *alone*, Robinson!" Dominic yelled, staggering to his feet.

"Shut up!" Eric turned his attention back to Anna. "Didn't you *miss* me, sweetheart?" He stuck his hand inside her bra and fondled her roughly. "Or were you too busy fucking his brains out to care?"

Anna glared at the man who was once her husband. He was a monster. "You're disgusting and vile. Any man, I don't care who, would be a damn sight better than *you*. You're *scum*, Eric. You make my flesh *crawl*."

Eric slapped her viciously. "You filthy whore! I *never* loved you.

I just *used* you to get what I wanted…a meal ticket. You were a *boring,* uptight lay in the sack, and a *fucking* nag!" he raged.

He turned to Dominic. "Here's the deal. I want you to wire ten million dollars into an offshore account. I'll give you all the instructions you need. If you don't, I *will* kill her. She means nothing to me. But before I do, I'll let Sheldon do 'er."

Sheldon smacked his lips together. "I can't wait to jam it to her, she's gonna be *beggin'* for it."

Dominic clenched his fists. "I shoulda killed you all those years ago, you fuckin' ugly freak."

Eric interrupted. "Now, now, Dominic. I'd hold my tongue if I were you. You don't want Anna here to find out our little secret do you? 'Cause I sure as hell know you didn't tell her squat about our history."

"What's he talking about Dominic?"

Dominic looked at Anna. "Are you okay?" he asked helplessly.

Her left cheek had a nasty purple bruise on it from where Eric had struck her. Her lower lip was cut at the corner. Her face was pale and tense. She was scared out of her mind.

"Did they touch you, Anna?" God, if they raped her, he'd lose it. "Sweetheart, did either one of them *touch* you?"

She shook her head, tears dripped off her chin. "No," she whispered. "Oh, Dominic, I'm *so* sorry," she sobbed. "He *made* me call you…tell you all those horrible lies. It's all my fault…"

"How *very* touching, Anna," Eric interrupted with a sneer. "Tell me, did Prince Charming here tell you that I used to date his sister?" he asked with a challenge.

"Shut the fuck up," warned Dominic.

Eric ignored him. "Jenny was her name and man-oh-man, was she a juicy little piece. Fucked her good too, until the dumb cunt got herself knocked up."

Dominic turned white with fury and took a half step towards Eric. Eric cocked the .357. "Don't even *think* about movin', friend, all it'll take is one little squeeze and…BOOM!" he shouted. "Her brains are splattered all over the place."

Anna flinched and held back a sob. She was tied up and helpless.

"Now where *was* I? Oh yeah, the bitch got pregnant and she expected *me* to play daddy. I told her what a worthless, stupid slut she was and beat it outta there."

He glared at Dominic. "And I wasn't alone either. I had a hot-lookin' babe with me." He laughed with malice. "I even told her to go kill herself. Man," he shook his head. "The bitch *was* a doormat 'cause she went out and did it!" he hooted.

Dominic didn't even remember crossing the room. He was in Eric's face in the blink of an eye. He punched the gun out of his hand and it went flying, skidding across the floor. With a roar, he picked Eric up by his neck and shook him like a rag doll.

"You're dead," he rasped.

He began squeezing his neck. Eric clawed at Dominic's forearms, but his hand was like a steel vise.

Anna struggled violently and worked her hand free from the rope. She quickly untied herself, oblivious to her bleeding wrists and ankles. She was on the verge of hysteria, making little animal noises at the back of her throat.

Eve screeched at Sheldon. "Fuckin' *DO* something!"

Sheldon, who was watching spellbound, suddenly sprang in to action. He scrambled around to the left and brought his gun up. He fired haphazardly.

The bullet struck Dominic's shoulder. He grunted in pain, dropping Eric on reflex. Eric lay on the ground coughing and gasping for air. Dominic clutched his shoulder and fell to his knees. He'd lost a lot of blood; his face was white and perspiring.

Anna ran to his side, cradling him in her arms. "Dominic!" she sobbed. She looked up at Eric. "God *damn* you to hell, Eric! You deserve to *die* for all the pain you've caused!"

Eric staggered to his feet and glared at Sheldon. "Gimme your gun," he rasped.

Sheldon passed him his gun. "It's about *time*. Blow the motherfucker away," he chanted.

Eric took the gun and aimed it at Sheldon's head. "Oh, I intend to."

Sheldon took a faltering step back. "What the fuck…?"

Eric glared at him with disgust. "You didn't really think I was gonna blow Lockwood away without gettin' my money first did you?"

"No, Eric," Sheldon held his hands up. "I just…"

Eric interrupted him. "And you *really* didn't think I'd share it with a mutant like *you,* did you? Especially since you didn't do *dick* to help me while I was being choked to death! If Eve hadn't of snapped you out of it, I'd be dead. You're a useless dumb-ass, Leevy. You always were."

He pulled the trigger and blew a hole right through Sheldon's wandering eye.

Anna screamed, covering Dominic with her body. As weak as he was, he flipped her over so his body was sheltering hers.

Eric stepped over Sheldon's body and strode over to Eve, kissing her hard. "Thanks, baby. I knew I could count on you."

Eve lightly scratched her nails down his cheek. "You always can," she purred. *As long as you get the money.*

Anna glared at them. "You both make me *sick*."

Eve cut her eyes to her. "Fuck *you*, bitch," she snapped.

"Go to hell!" Anna shouted. "You're *nothing* but garbage. A poor imitation of a human being!"

"Why you little…" Eve lunged toward her. Dominic was on his feet in an instant. He shoved Anna behind him.

"*Touch* her and see what happens," he snarled.

Eve backed quickly away and stood next to Eric. Lockwood's eyes were flat. He looked like he would kill her in an instant if he had the chance.

Eric draped his arm over Eve's shoulders. "Don't waste your time on *her*, baby. She's not worth it. Anna is the most stupid, gullible loser on earth. Isn't that right, Anna? You believed everything that came outta my mouth. It was really such a *shame* you didn't listen to your old bitch of a mother. I sure fixed her though." He laughed cagily.

Anna's face was leeched of all color. "What are you talking about, Eric," she whispered. The room was deathly quiet.

"Eric, give me the information and you'll get your money," Dominic interrupted. He had a sick feeling in his stomach, and he wanted to spare Anna the pain. "You let Anna walk out of here and I'll make it fifteen million."

Anna was oblivious to everything except her ex-husband. "What do you *mean* you took care of her?" She trembled.

"Anna. Please, honey, let it *go*," whispered Dominic urgently.

"No, Dominic," she said fiercely. "I want to know."

Eric's eyes were alight with venom. "Your mama's death was *no* accident."

Anna sucked in her breath sharply. Dominic braced her against himself. "You animal," he rasped, knowing what was coming next.

Eric continued. "I waited outside the condo until she came out for work. I followed her and ran her off Miller Road. I did you a favor though; I made sure she went off that cliff. She died on impact and probably didn't feel a thing." He laughed. "Except for the few seconds it took her to hit the bottom, I imagine she was shitting bricks then."

Eve ran her tongue over her lips and laughed bitchily.

Anna felt the blood roar in her ears. She twisted away from Dominic and threw herself at Eric, with her fingernails drawn. She pushed him over and sat on top of his chest. Anna took advantage of his surprise and knocked Sheldon's pistol out of his hand.

She raked her nails across his right eye and down his face, leaving four bloody-red grooves that ended at his chin. He screamed and flung her off of him. Anna tumbled and struck her head against the pavement.

Dominic kicked Eric in the gut. "C'mon, get up." He kicked him again, this time harder. "I said get the *fuck* up! It's you an' me now."

Eric rolled to his feet, wiping the blood from his eye. They circled around each other.

Dominic had his hands up around his face. There was a bloodstain the size of a dinner plate on his left shoulder. He stepped forward and with his fist, jabbed Eric in the face.

Eric's head snapped back. He swung and wildly clipped Dominic in his injured shoulder.

He grunted and did a quick combination. He landed a hard punch to his nose and a swift uppercut to his kidneys. Eric dropped to his knees and clutched his stomach.

Dominic jumped in the air and kicked him in the head, knocking him out flat. His body flew a couple of feet before smacking the ground with a dull thud.

Dominic stood over him breathing harshly. The deafening sound of a gun blast pierced the air. Dominic spun around. Anna was on her knees with Eve standing behind her. She had the gun pressed hard against the back of Anna's head.

# Chapter Forty-Two

Eve's eyes were like ice. "Let's stop with the dramatics, shall we? I mean, just about everyone's had a gun pressed against this bitch's head. The only difference is *I* have the balls to shoot."

Dominic didn't doubt her for an instant. "Fine. Let her go and we'll deal."

Eve smiled nastily. "Whatever you say, lover."

She hit Anna on the side of the head with the barrel. Anna dropped like a stone and lay deathly still.

"Anna!" Dominic screamed.

Eric opened his eyes. Dominic had his back to him. He spotted the Magnum. It was lying just out of his reach. He began crawling towards it.

Eve held the gun steady. "Now you and I are going to take a little ride. She'll come with me in one car and you'll go in another. That way I know you won't fuck me over. Then you're gonna make a fifteen-million-dollar transfer into my account."

"I thought it was Eric's account," sneered Dominic, stalling for time.

"Eric could be dead for I'll I care. He's nothing but a pathetic loser. The money is mine now. *All* mine."

"You fuckin' *traitor*!" Eric shouted.

Dominic had just enough time to spin around and drop to the ground.

Eric blew a one-foot hole in the middle of Eve's stomach. The impact of the blast threw her body back against the wall. She slid down it, leaving a wet, bloody trail of bone and guts.

Dominic rolled to his feet. He put himself in front of Anna's prone body.

195

Eric staggered to his. "It's time to die now, Lockwood." He cocked the trigger.

Nick Rossi sprinted to Eric's left. His brown eyes were like flint. He focused on his target. He crossed in front of Eric and emptied his gun into him. Eric squeezed off a shot, but Rossi rolled to the ground, missing the bullet by an inch.

Eric's body lay crumpled on the pavement. Rossi stood over him and kicked the gun out of his hand. He squatted down and pressed his two fingers against his throat.

Eric Robinson was very dead.

"OOOH *NOOO!*" Anna was screaming, crawling towards Dominic frantically.

"Sweet *Jesus!*" exclaimed Nick.

He scrambled over to his friend. Dominic lay unconscious. His big, powerful body looked strangely vulnerable.

Eric's bullet had grazed Dominic's chest. There was a deep valley where the bullet ripped through his flesh. He was bleeding profusely. Blood seeped from his head and shoulder as well.

"Please, *please* help him!" Anna sobbed hysterically. "Don't let him die, please. I can't *lose* him. Not now…we just *found* each other. *Please…*"

Nick clamped his hand down on the wound and, with the other, fumbled with his radio. "This is Inspector Nick Rossi. I need a MediVac chopper at 357 Lakeside Avenue *now!*" he said harshly.

"The victim has gunshot wounds to the chest and shoulder. You're gonna have to send in the homicide and crime scene units. We got two…no…*three* people dead. Hurry!"

Anna had Dominic's head on her lap. She was rocking him and humming softly, pausing only to kiss him gently on face. "I love you," she whispered.

Nick applied pressure to Dominic's chest and said his prayers.

He hoped his friend would live.

# *Epilogue*

### *Eighteen Months Later*

The Hampton estate was a riot in color. Flowering trees were in full bloom. Gardenias, roses, and honeysuckle made the limpid summer air heady.

The huge back lawn was a deep emerald green. Dominic was stretched out on his stomach and under attack.

Eight-month-old Nicholas Lockwood, named after his doting godfather, was bouncing on his father's broad back. He had two chubby fistfuls of Dominic's hair clutched in his hands. He was gurgling with glee as he attempted to scalp his daddy. Dominic felt a glob of drool hit his forehead. It rolled into his eyebrow.

"Ugh," he groaned. "Baby spit!" It only made Nicky giggle louder and yank harder.

Little Nick's fraternal twin, Jennifer Abigail Lockwood or, Abby as she was nicknamed, was sitting on top of a soft blanket industriously chewing on her shoe, which she had cleverly managed to wiggle off her tiny foot.

Dominic was convinced she was a genius.

He loved his wife and children with an intensity that was almost frightening. He'd never been so utterly and completely happy in his life.

He thought back to that terrible day he'd almost lost Anna. They'd flown him to a trauma center and had to perform emergency surgery to remove the bullet lodged in his shoulder. They gave him two blood transfusions and hoped for the best.

He regained consciousness in the ICU twelve hours later. Anna was right by his side when his eyes fluttered open.

"Hi," she softly said. She touched his face with a trembling hand. Tears were bright in her eyes. She was pale and wan. Dominic had never seen her looking so beautiful.

"Hi yourself," he whispered. He was surprised to hear how weak he sounded. He scanned her face. "Are you okay, honey? Oh God, your head." He reached up to lightly touch the stitches on her temple. "I'm sorry, Anna. I…I couldn't protect you," he said in frustration. His eyes filled with tears.

Anna leaned down and kissed his eyelids. "Shh…" she whispered. "Don't you *know*, Dominic? You saved my life when you first walked through my door. I was empty and alone and scared. I was only half-alive. You swooped in and took me to your beautiful castle, and I was lost. As much as I tried to fight it, you pushed your way into my heart." She laughed shakily. "Remember the wild story you spun about crazy old Agatha?"

He nodded and laughed a little. "If I recall, you were scared stiff."

"Yes. Yes I was. Until I realized you were pulling my leg. And when you laughed…I don't know, it was with your whole heart and you looked…so free and young.

"You were beautiful. You took my breath away, and I haven't recovered yet. I don't think I ever will. I love you, Dominic. I *love* you. I always will, until the day I die." She kissed him softly on his mouth.

He laced his fingers through her hair and kissed her passionately. "This bed's lonely," he complained. "I'm gonna need you to slide in next to me if there's any hope of me making a full recovery."

Anna gazed at him mischievously. "What about the nurses? They look fierce." She carefully lay down next to him, cuddling against his side.

Dominic groaned. She felt so damn good. "Don't worry, baby, I'll sic you on 'em. They won't stand a chance," he said weakly.

She giggled. "Damn straight."

"Anna?"

"Hmm?"

"I love you."

\*\*\*\*\*\*\*\*\*

Over the next several days, Dominic told Anna everything. Eric had destroyed his sister. Murdered her beloved mother, and almost killed the both of them. He deserved everything Dominic had done to him. She felt no sorrow over his death. He was burning in hell where he belonged.

Dominic explained that when a colleague in the Mexican government contacted him about Eric's escape, and the murder of a guard and inmate, he knew it was a matter of time before he surfaced.

"That's when I knew I had to get you out of that house. I knew that Eric would contact you. I led him to believe that I was going to take you *and* that I'd have an affair with you. I knew that would burn in his gut. So I banked on him making a move. But believe me, Anna; under *no* circumstances would I have sacrificed you to him. No matter who you were.

"I didn't know when he'd show, but when he did, I was going to get rid of him, once and for all.

"Only I didn't count on falling madly in love," he said wryly. "I thought you were just like him, a cold and calculating criminal. I didn't know you were just as much of a victim of Eric's cruelty as Jenny was."

Anna brought his hand up to her lips and kissed it. She understood and forgave him for believing the worst. He did it with the most noble of intentions.

"And now?" she wanted to know.

He smiled. "And now it's happily ever after time. I love you Anna…totally and forever. You're my soul mate. I've been searching my whole life for you, only I didn't know it. You make my life worth living. Please, *please,* marry me and make me the happiest man alive. I know I'm not the easiest person to get along with, but I'll spend the rest of my life making you happy. I *swear* it on my life."

She nodded breathlessly and wrapped her arms around him, laughing and crying at the same time.

They were married three weeks later at the Hampton estate. It was small and beautiful; William gave the bride away. Nick was the best man and Katherine was the matron of honor. They felt very blessed.

**********

Dominic scooped his baby son from around his neck and tickled him until he squealed. He did the same with little Abby. He loved them. They were the very best part of him.

He felt his sister's love surrounding him. He no longer thought about her and felt a debilitating sense of loss. The memories were warm and comforting. He was finally able to let her rest in peace.

He looked up and grinned when he saw Anna approaching with a soft smile on her face. She was barefoot and wore a filmy white summer dress. She was tan, fit and incredibly lovely. His breath caught in his throat and his heart skipped a beat.

She was his heart and soul.

The beautiful mother of his children. He felt so lucky, so wonderfully light and happy. Dominic finally had his family.

He was home.

Printed in the United States
21803LVS00001B/497